D0513124

WITHDRAWN
FOR BOOKSALE

THE KILLING KIND

Jim Bartlett thought he could put his past behind him and forge a new life in Texas, as a small ranch owner — but he was wrong . . . dead wrong. Someone from his past has followed him and is systematically trying to destroy his new life, piece by piece. With his friends and the woman he loves being threatened by a man who knows no remorse, Jim struggles desperately — not only to escape his past — but also to hold onto his life . . .

LANCE HOWARD

THE KILLING KIND

Complete and Unabridged

LINFORD
Leicester

First published in Great Britain in 2010 by
Robert Hale Limited
London

First Linford Edition
published 2012
by arrangement with
Robert Hale Limited
London

British Library CIP Data

Howard, Lance.
 The killing kind. - - (Linford western library)
 1. Ranchers- -Texas- -Fiction. 2. Western
 stories. 3. Large type books.
 I. Title II. Series
 813.6–dc23

 ISBN 978–1–4448–1060–8

Published by
F. A. Thorpe (Publishing)
Anstey, Leicestershire

Set by Words & Graphics Ltd.
Anstey, Leicestershire
Printed and bound in Great Britain by
T. J. International Ltd., Padstow, Cornwall

For Tannenbaum.

*Please visit Lance Howard
on the web at:
www.howardhopkins.com*

1

When the man in the gray duster stepped into the general store, it seemed as if all light vanished within. Although morning sunlight blazed through the front window, flies and dust waltzing within its glowing shafts, the store interior appeared to darken. It was as if darkness gathered about the man.

He wore a battered hat, which had a chip missing on its brim and was pulled low to shadow the features of its wearer. Two years back, many a man in Colorado Territory would have testified as to how the man blackened a room just by his entry, but that was now the stuff of tall tales in cheap magazines that sold a legend that never was. Or, at least, was not yet ended.

The bell above the door chimed at his entrance. That was strangely ironic, he thought, because its cheerful ring foretold death. He was one for irony, and this mission, this task for which he had strived over the past two years, was as ironic an undertaking as any could get. The Dead bringing death.

Folks in Colorado made mistakes in their perceptions of outlaws, much the way those pulp writers did. They claimed them ignorant, the product of bad upbringings or loose brains.

But he was no such man. He was intelligent, crafty, and his parents, up until the time he put them in their graves, had seen fit to raise him properly. Bless them. It made plans easier to think through, and men easier to control, to frighten. Stupid men gave no thought to the game, to the satisfaction of drawing blood in a thin steady stream instead of splattering it everywhere, though he had been accused of his share of splattering, and rightly so.

Yet, still, while he was a damn sight smarter than the average owlhoot and considerably deadlier, no one here in the Texas panhandle knew him, no one in Wendell, except for two men who would never be expecting him. The notion brought a whispered laugh to his lips.

With his rearing, he had no excuse for the man he had become, other than he had just been born defective, corrupt; that suited him right fine. He needed no excuses for his actions. Never had, and never would. He was what he was: a mean-spirited bastard.

After closing the door behind him, the bell chiming again, he stepped deeper into the general store, the fall of his boots hollow, akin to thunder.

Two women, old, gray hair pulled high and tight beneath little round hats, turned their gazes toward him. Their wrinkled faces pinched at the sight of him as if, backlit by the light from the window, he was some sort of demon who'd simply materialized within the store. Their faded gingham dresses hung like rags on their bony frames and they gave him an up and down appraisal that brought disgust and a measure of fear to their red-seamed eyes. Blue-veined hands with skin like onion paper tightened on handbags and he might have chuckled had the irritation of finding them in the store not been prickling his hide. He had watched the entryway long enough and had judged the store empty, save for the man he had come to see. The two old women presented a problem, but fortunately one for which he had a solution. The same solution that solved all his ills: death.

They started to scuttle along a row of stacked canned goods and his head lifted slightly, signaling them to a stop without a word. One of them let out a small sound, like that of a mouse ground beneath a boot-heel. It pleased him.

His gray eyes swept over the small place, scanning its aisles of shelves stocked with colored bottles of various elixirs and canned goods, sacks of oats and flour piled high on the floor, barrels

4

standing near a low counter flanking the right wall.

'Where is he?' the man asked, his gaze shifting to the counter. 'Where's Jess Henley?'

'W-who?' one of the women said, almost a chirp.

'Calls himself Billy Fredericks now . . .' he said, forgetting for a moment the stupid bastard had changed his name to prevent just what was about to happen.

'In . . . in the back,' the other old woman said, her voice worn, as frail as her appearance.

'He went to fetch us something . . .' the first one said, voice quivering.

'Your cooperation won't save you,' he said.

He realized it wasn't only his presence and the evil they might have felt emanating from him that brought about their nervousness. Something else was making them antsy. He surmised the storekeep had gone to fetch them liquor of some kind; that's why they had likely snuck in here through the back and he hadn't seen them enter. For some reason unknown to him, these ladies were hiding their vice. Everyone had their secrets, didn't they? From the prissiest churchgoer to the orneriest outlaw. But they all had one thing in common: they rarely died with them. Secrets had a way of spilling out.

A sound from the back caught his attention. His head lifted a fraction and strands of brown straggly hair showed in the arc of sunlight that sliced through the store window. Momentarily, a small portion of his lower face was revealed and one of the old women let out a startled yelp.

'You damn well best shut it,' he said, cocking his head back to her. He couldn't blame her for her reaction. She'd likely never seen a man with scars such as his: a dead man's scars.

Coming from the back, clutching two bottles of amber liquor, the storekeep pulled up short. The bleat from the old woman had halted his entry and he peered at the stranger in the duster as if the Devil himself had stepped into his parlor.

Indeed, that was damn near the truth of the matter, thought the man. 'Everyone loves a surprise, don't they, Henley?' he said, his voice low, raspy.

'No . . . ' the storekeep said, barely audible. 'It ain't possible.'

'Anything's possible, Henley, you should know that. Except for maybe killing a ghost.'

The storekeeper's fear delighted him much more than even he had anticipated. The little runt of a man with a shock of blonde-brown hair quivered like a kitten.

The women started moving towards the door again.

'We'll just come back later for our . . . medicine . . . ' one said, pushing the other ahead of her a step.

A whiff of a flowery odor assailed his nostrils. It came from the women, sickening, like lilies at a funeral. He detested that stench, detested old people in general and the way they stank of death's approaching corruption.

'You aren't going anywhere,' he said, head tilting back to them, and the women stopped again.

'Please . . . ' the 'keep said. 'Let them go . . . '

'Beg your God, Henley, though I doubt He'll listen any better than I would. Or care a lick more.'

'We got a new life now,' the store owner said, still quaking. His eyes had widened and sweat trickled down his face.

'You reckon? You reckon you can run far enough from your old one?' The man paused, the flowery scent annoying him further, making his hand itch to go for the Smith & Wesson at his hip to add the acrid scent of gunpowder to the mix.

The storekeeper shook his head. 'We wasn't runnin'. We was just tryin' to start over, make amends.' The owner swallowed hard, his prominent Adam's apple doing a dance.

'You were always just a follower,

Henley, but Bartlett, he was a trouble-maker. Reckon it was all his idea?'

The 'keep nodded like a rabbit, though it was plain it was simply a nervous reaction and not a betrayal. 'Please just go. We won't never tell anyone.'

The man laughed, an unpleasant sound that brought another squeak from one of the old women.

'I told you to shut it,' the man said, looking back to them, and suddenly the gun was in his hand. The old women's eyes widened and their trembling increased.

'No!' the 'keep said. 'Please don't . . . Just leave.'

'Oh, I'm leaving, Henley. Don't you worry any about that. For you, it'll be quick, but for Bartlett . . . he's gonna learn there's no escaping who . . . *what* I am.'

The 'keep started to back up, but the man's Smith & Wesson swung to aim and thunder filled the store. The thunder was followed by the sound of bottles shattering as they hit the floorboards and the screams of the two old women.

Those screams ended a heartbeat later, but the thunder did not.

2

Six hours earlier . . .

Shards of lightning sizzled through
charcoal-colored clouds. Their under-
bellies bloated, they readied to release a
torrent of rain across the wind-whipped
fields of buffalo grass. The odor of
damp earth and sin saturated the air.

Sudden crashes of sound echoed
around Jim Bartlett as he stood in the
vast night drenched field. Dressed only
in his union suit, the wind snapped at
him like hungry coyotes, sent chills
shuddering through his wiry frame and
whipped about his sandy brown hair.
The ghost of a scar on his left cheek
seemed to throb.

At first, he perceived the sounds to
be thunder, but the staccato booms
occurred in rapid succession, sometimes three, four at a time. And with

each crash he jolted, as if invisible bullets had punched through his chest and back, knocking him backward, then forward. Yet when he peered down at his chest no blood showed beside the undergarment's row of buttons, no holes marred the sweat-stained cloth.

With the gunshot thunder ululated high-pitched squeals, mingled with the frantic bawling of cattle. Then laughter rode the chilled wind; damning laughter, accusing laughter.

With a blink, bodies lay sprawled among the gale-whipped blades, each with wide open eyes, dead eyes, and blood-spattered faces.

And he knew then this storm's makeup, its origin: it was a tempest of conscience, a black norther of guilt.

He's coming . . .

'No!' he shouted, his voice carrying above the howl of the wind.

Laughter again. Closer. Louder. More brutal.

'I didn't kill them!' he yelled, jamming his hands against his ears to repel the accusing laughter. Sweat streamed from his brow and ran down his face.

You didn't stop him . . .

'I couldn't!' His face rose to the gray-black swollen sky, a plea of forgiveness in his brown eyes. But the night, the storm, appeared indifferent.

Peals of laughter penetrated his hands, ears, drove into his brain.

You cannot escape who you are . . .

'Damn you!' he yelled, hands dropping from his ears. He balled a fist, shook it at the night as he fell to his knees. 'I won't take your blame! I won't let you haunt me anymore!'

You . . . have . . . no . . . choice. . . .

With an enormous roar, the clouds burst. But what fell, though icy and wet, was not rain. For it came in dime-sized drops that painted the grass with scarlet and bathed him in blame —

'No!' Jim Bartlett said, jutting straight up in bed. His heart trip-hammered against his ribs and sweat streamed down his face, his chest, from beneath his arms.

His breath beat out in jerky gasps and his calloused hands shook as he buried his face in his palms.

It was not the first time he'd suffered with the nightmare. He should have gotten used to it by now.

But this time the dream felt different, more ominous somehow, almost . . . a warning.

For the last two years his past, his former life and deeds, had stalked him. Lord knew, he'd done his damnedest to outrun them, and to make up for them. But they couldn't be outrun, nor atoned for, could they? Because those deeds, what he had been, dwelled inside his very soul. And a body could never escape its own conscience.

Different. Something else had changed too. What?

He was damned if he knew but he trembled like a newborn calf and that reaction, at least, was not like him. In many ways he was still a hard man, though he prayed, a changed one.

You can't escape . . .

A shudder. He sighed, withdrew his face from his hands and peered into the darkness of his bedroom. Dusky outlines of a dresser holding a porcelain basin and pitcher glazed with tiny powder-blue flowers that Emma had given to him, a night table and wingbacked chair met his gaze. Moonlight, as stark as glowing skulls, sliced through the French doors and across the scuffed wooden floor.

He drew a deep breath, swung his legs out of bed and came to his feet. His legs trembled so badly he worried he might collapse right back on to the feather bed. Fighting back the residual nerves, he saddled his composure enough to walk a stiff line to the French doors. Gripping the handles tight enough to turn his knuckles bone white in the moonlight, he hesitated, almost afraid of what he might discover beyond them, then pulled the doors open.

As he stepped out on to the balcony, night air, brisk, swept over him and he shuddered again.

No storm, he told himself as he reached the edge of the balcony and leaned heavily against the rail for support.

Moonlight bathed the ranch compound grounds, glazed grassy swales and gentle rolling hills in the distance, and highlighted in bone-colored relief the myriad outbuildings — icehouse, bunkhouse, barn — and corral. Everything appeared serene and the breeze hushed like ladies whispering rumors through the leaves of scattered stands of cottonwoods peppering the field.

Secrets. Secrets lived here; his secrets. They dwelled in this place and festered within him.

Movement near a stand of cottonwoods captured his attention and for a heartbeat a figure in a dark duster stood there, peering up at the balcony. Jim's belly plunged and he blinked. The figure was gone. Had he truly seen it, or had it been merely an illusion left over from his dream?

That had to be the explanation. No

one lurked near the trees. No one who could have come back to haunt him, because the person he thought he had seen was long dead.

And dead men did not return from the grave.

* * *

When the sun turned the morning sky to blood, Jim Bartlett was still gazing out at the field. He hadn't been able to go back to sleep, too shaken by the nightmare and by guilt from his past. He wondered if he'd ever truly escape what he'd done. Perhaps not. Perhaps the dream was right: there was no escape.

But there was a future in which he did his best to make amends. That was one of the reasons he served as part-time deputy in Wendell, as well as owned this small cattle ranch. To make things right, to help those who needed it. He didn't know what else he could do.

There's nothing else. You killed him — avenged those who died.

The glimpse of the dark figure in the field ran through his mind again, accompanied by a chill. It was just a vision left over from his nightmare, he assured himself. Just his own dark conscience. It had to be.

Then why do you feel that something evil's out there, waiting?

That was a good question, and one for the moment he had to chalk up to lack of sleep and a bridle of paranoia he'd carried with him ever since the day he left Colorado.

That's enough thinking on that time, he chastised himself, shaking his head. *That time was in the past. Gone. Forever.*

That's all there was to it.

He pushed himself away from the railing and gazed out at the compound once more. He noticed smoke spiraling from the bunkhouse, where his two men, his foreman, Jakes, and a younger fellow named Hicks had already arisen to start the day. The sun still painted the fields with a gory cast but the scarlet was mellowing to rose.

He went into his room, sighed, heaviness settling over him, making his limbs feel like lead and his soul like iron. He couldn't keep going without sleep, not with ranch and law work to be done.

On top of that, there was Emma, whom he hoped to ask to marry him someday. Over the past months, since they'd become serious, he had been hesitating. He loved her; he was certain of that much. He looked forward to every moment they spent together, yet . . .

Fear stopped him from taking that final step. If she knew he had been lying to her, what he had been . . .

You can't wait forever.

No, he couldn't, because if he didn't ask her one day soon he would find her gone and have only himself to blame.

He went to the bureau and poured water into the basin from the pitcher.

After splashing his face, he toweled off on an old shirt draped over the wingbacked chair, then located a boiled shirt and shrugged it on. Trousers and boots followed, and a blue bandanna around his neck.

He went out into the hall, greeted by the scent of smoky bacon and rich Arbuckle's. Mrs Pendergast was already preparing the morning meal and the familiar scents comforted him a measure, though he didn't feel much like eating. He swore the old woman, always up at the crack of dawn, slept less than he did.

He descended the stairs, the leaden feeling in his legs staying with him. Sunlight, now a golden color, arced through the parlor windows and fell across a modest sofa, old chairs and a writing table. The ranchhouse appeared as peaceful as on any other morning, and the field beyond the windows was serene under the new dawn.

The dining room was also unpretentiously furnished: a long-beamed table and chairs, standing buffet, chandelier and little else. At the moment only he and Mrs Pendergast lived in the house, which had four other unused bedrooms, and he had given little thought to decoration in the two years he'd occupied it. He reckoned Emma could change that; Lord knew the place needed a woman's touch. Mrs Pendergast was too old to bother with such things, other than keeping it clean and her cooking duties.

'You look like hell,' came a voice from the end of the table, and he nodded to his foreman, Jakes, who stood with his hat in hand.

'Reckon I was never a lovely sight at any time of day,' he said, taking a seat. The foreman slid out a chair, turned it about, then straddled it.

''Cept you look worse than usual. You could put those bags under your eyes on your saddle. More nightmares?'

He nodded, having little desire to discuss it. 'Nothing new.'

The foreman's weathered brow cinched and he cast Jim a look that said he didn't believe a word of it. 'Care to tell me about them yet?'

'Past's best left buried, Jakes. Some things ain't never meant to be spoken of again.'

'Unless those things eat you up inside, boy.' Jakes peered at him. The man was a good ten years his senior, almost a father figure in some ways. Gray peppered the man's scrubby beard and temples, and a lick of black hair hung over the right side of his forehead. Jakes was a tough man; Jim could tell that the moment he set eyes on him and he suspected a story lay somewhere behind that, but he had never seen fit to ask. It was Jakes' business, just as his own past belonged to him.

'It'll die down eventually,' Jim said, little conviction in his tone.

'You sure 'bout that?' Jakes cocked an eyebrow.

'I'm sure,' he said, the lie obvious in his voice.

Jakes glanced out the window. 'Hicks is already out tending to that fence on the far pasture. Got a lot of sap for a young'un.'

Jim chuckled. 'Young'un'? He's near old as I am.'

Jakes smiled. 'That makes him a young'un, least from my perspective.' The foreman paused, then looked intently at Jim. 'You know, I never really told you what brought me here lookin' for a job, did I?'

'You don't have to. Your record's spotless as far as I'm concerned. Anything in the past is your own business.'

'Maybe my work record . . . ' The foreman hesitated, sighed. 'But not the record that's gonna count when the Good Lord comes callin' for me.'

'We all got our faults . . . ' He avoided the man's gaze, shifted in his chair and wished the old woman would hurry up with their breakfast. He reached for the blue-enameled coffee pot in the center of the table and poured Arbuckle's into the cup Mrs Pendergast had set out for him.

'I need to be straight with you, boy,'

Jakes said. 'It's been weighin' on my mind. See, time was when I was as like to steal cattle as help raise them.'

Jim nodded. He had suspected something like that. The man had come to him a year and a half ago, as knowledgeable as anyone he'd ever met when it came to longhorns. He hadn't questioned the man's past or credentials — what right, given his own history, did he have to do that? What mattered was the job the man had done for two years and never once had Jim glimpsed any hint of shifty behavior.

After taking a sip of coffee, Jim set the cup down. 'You probably ain't telling me anything I haven't figured out.'

Jakes nodded. 'Still, best I lay it out. I owe you that. You took a chance on a stranger — '

'A stranger with a hell of a lot of know-how when it came to cattle.'

''Cause I used to help steal them and alter brands, then sell them off cheap to other ranches and Injuns. I ain't proud of what I done. Don't even think for a moment I'm telling you to brag. I'm telling you because it's been on my conscience and I have done my best for this past year or more to make up for my sins. Ain't no excuse, but I was raised by a drunken pa and he went and got his ass kilt one night and never came home. I had to learn to survive on my own and I did. But I always recollected this one lady, at the church, who was kind to me. I never thought much about her when my pa died and for a while after. Then one day I did, and I thought about how she had tried to help me when I came to her all beat up by his fool drunken hand.'

'And that turned you around? Something that small?'

Jakes nodded. ''Cept it wasn't small in the scheme of things. It was a seed planted that grew into something bigger than I ever expected. Point is, I saw what I was doing was wrong and decided I didn't want to be that man no more.'

Jim stared at the table, his gaze

tracing the swirls and creases in the white linen. 'Both my parents died of consumption when I was young. I got bounced around a lot. Lost my way . . . '
He stopped, catching himself, knowing he had revealed more than he wanted to to the foreman, but weary of holding everything inside.

'I reckon I know.'

'All I'm saying is it don't matter what you done in the past. Matters what you do now.' Jim hoped steering the subject to the present would prevent the foreman from questioning him any further about the past.

'I knew no rancher in their right mind would hire a former brand artist, even a greenhorn rancher such as your ownself, so I didn't tell you when I came here looking for a job.'

'So why tell me now?'

''Cause like I said, it's been weighin' on my conscience and I need it off my mind. I figure I proved myself as much as a man can do.'

Jim nodded. 'And more. Couldn't

run this spread, even small as it is, without you.'

'I'm also telling you 'cause I see what's happening to you, how the guilt of something you done in the past is eating you up. I know those nightmares are getting to you. If you need to talk, I'll understand it, whatever it is.'

He took another sip of his coffee, frowned, then looked at Jakes, eyes narrowing a fraction as he set down his cup. 'You might not understand, Jakes. Or you might. I don't know. But it isn't just guilt that's got hold of me, it's something . . . else.'

'What?'

He shrugged. 'I ain't sure exactly.'

'It's the Devil, that's what it is!' came a shrill voice behind him. He swung his head to see Mrs Pendergast entering the room with two plates heaped with scrambled eggs, bacon and fried potatoes. Frail of form, she shuffled to the table like an animated skeleton. She set a plate before him, then slid the other in front of Jakes. Her thin hands, rivered with blue veins, shook with a permanent tremble and her gaunt face looked like parchment-thin skin drawn tight over bone. Dark gullies pooled beneath her lusterless gray eyes and her thin gray hair was pulled back in a tight bun that alleviated the skull impression not in the least.

'What are you babbling about now, woman?' Jakes asked, digging into his food. Jim reckoned Jakes ate as much as any two men yet somehow remained scarecrow thin.

'The Devil was here last night, Mr Bartlett,' she said, her eyes darting.

'What are you talking about?' he asked, not liking the sinking feeling in his belly.

'Out in the field.' With a thin hand she made a waving motion towards the far window. 'I saw him, just a-standin' there, he was. All Devillike.'

Jakes frowned. 'Devillike?'

'Well, I couldn't rightly see his face but he was dark and mean lookin'.'

Jakes uttered an unkind laugh and

the old woman gave him a scowl. 'Couldn't see his face but he was mean lookin'?' the foreman said. 'Foolishness. Nobody out there last night.' He shoveled a forkful of eggs into his mouth.

Jim looked across the room and out through the window into the yard beyond. He had passed the figure off as a leftover figment of his nightmare, but that nightmare couldn't have affected two people at the same time. He pushed his plate away, what little appetite he might have mustered deserting him.

★ ★ ★

'You know she's a crazy old woman, right?' Jakes said twenty minutes later, hoisting a coil of rope on to the top rail of the corral.

Jim stood looking out across the field, realizing he had gotten lost in thought. But he couldn't help it. Had he seen someone standing out there last night? Surely not the Devil, but who?

'She saw something . . . ' Jim muttered, then licked his lips. The sun had risen just above the horizon and its heat beat against his face. Sweat trickled from his brow. The breeze had warmed; the day would be another hot one.

Jakes scoffed. 'That old bat sees lots of things that ain't real, you know that. Don't know why you keep her ornery old bones around.'

Jim shrugged. 'Because she had nowhere else to go when her husband got killed. I felt sorry for her. She does fine cooking and cleaning.'

'And seeing ghosts.'

'Devils.'

'OK, devils, of which there ain't no such.'

'Except I might have seen him too.'

The foremen stopped uncoiling the rope. 'What?'

'Last night, after I woke up, I came out on to the balcony. Thought I saw a man standing out there, near that stand of cottonwood.' He ducked his chin at the trees.

'Any man in particular?'

He wanted to say a name but held back and he could tell the foreman knew it. 'Just a man . . . in a duster. Only got a glimpse. Wasn't sure it was real even. It was too dark to see his face.'

'Did you need to see his face?'

Jakes knew Jim had a name to go with whomever he had seen, and was pushing him to come out with it.

Jim shook his head, the sinking feeling returning to his belly. 'Just don't like it. If she saw him, too, then someone was out there.'

Jakes unconsciously looked out over the field. 'Why would someone be standing out in your field in the dead of night?'

'That's a damn good question.'

The foreman peered at Jim, studying him, the fact obvious: there was more to the story. Jim reckoned it was also obvious he had no inclination to talk about it further.

Fortunately, the choice was made for him. With a sudden thudding of hoofs, a rider came galloping in from the opposite end of the ranch compound. The horseman swung around the icehouse and headed straight for them.

'Hicks,' Jakes said, eyes narrowing beneath his battered felt hat.

Jim's own eyes narrowed — he didn't like the dread that came with that rider. The urgency in Hicks's approach warned him something was wrong, and he had a notion it was somehow connected to his nightmare and the figure he'd glimpsed in the field.

The man charged up to them, reined his horse to a halt, then peered down. Anxiousness played in his blue eyes and tightened his young face.

'What is it, Hicks?' Jim asked, not sure he wanted to hear the answer.

'You best saddle up and ride with me to the edge of the compound, Mr Bartlett, down near the gorge.'

'What happened?' Jakes asked. 'Rustlers?'

Hicks's head swung to the foreman. 'Best you see for yerself, Mr Jakes. I ain't never seen the like. Can't rightly believe it, but weren't no rustler, that's for damn sure.'

Jim nodded, frowned. He didn't like this, not one lick. First his nightmare, then someone standing in his field, now something else.

He had a sinking suspicion everything had just started coming apart around him and it was only the beginning.

3

'Godalmighty,' mumbled Jim as he reined to a halt near the gorge that flanked the west side of the property. Jakes drew up beside him, grizzled face somber, and Hicks pulled up on his right, his features tight with shock.

'What the hell?' Jakes said, surveying the scene before them.

'There's five more over to the south side,' Hicks said. 'Done the same way.'

Jim nodded, a stunned numbness washing over him. He sucked in a deep breath, nudged his hat up on his forehead and with his forearm sleeve wiped his brow. Not knowing the problem, he'd neglected to bring his gun, but it was probably too late for that. It occurred to him that whoever had done this had left the evidence as a warning and likely wasn't waiting in ambush.

As a precaution, his gaze swept across the land in every direction, seeking any possible hiding place for a man. There were damn few and he saw nothing. He had a notion whoever had committed this deed would know his reaction by heart and would be laughing about it, savoring it.

No, it's not possible . . .

It shouldn't have been possible, at any rate. Men simply did not come back from the dead.

'You got a notion who done this?'

He came from his thoughts to see Jakes staring at him and he knew suspicion must have shown on his face. He shook his head.

'No . . . ' he said with far less conviction than he would have liked.

'You say 'no' but your eyes say 'yes'.' Jakes stepped from the saddle. 'There's a threat out there, you best be telling me so I can prepare for it.'

'There's nothing.' Jim fought to put more confidence in his tone. 'There can't be.'

'Why's that?' Jakes looked up at him, doubt playing on his features.

'Because . . . ' He stopped himself. He'd been about to say something that would have required an explanation he had no wish to give.

Because he's dead . . .

'Because there's nothing,' Jim finished, his gaze going back to the scene before him.

'Cain't be rustlers,' Hicks said, shifting in his saddle.

Jim nodded, then dismounted. 'No, rustlers don't leave carcasses.' He walked over to the five dead longhorns sprawled in the graze, each abuzz with flies. An odor of death assailed his nostrils and his belly cinched.

'They all been shot through the head,' Jakes said, kneeling beside one of the dead animals. He let out a groan. 'This . . . this ain't normal.'

He's coming. . . .

No. . . .

Jim knelt beside one of the dead longhorns, barely able to look at the poor beast. He noted the bullet hole in the animal's skull and nausea clawed its way into his throat.

'No, it ain't normal,' Jim said. 'Not one damn bit.'

Jakes peered at him, face serious. 'Like you said, rustlers would have taken them, altered their brands. I got enough experience to know they wouldn't have just killed them animals and left them to rot. This is some kind of warning. A personal warning.'

Jim's head lifted and he stared straight ahead, at a loss for words. The foreman was right, but what could he say that didn't involve revealing things better left buried?

'Maybe one of the other ranches . . . ' he said, voice hesitant.

Jakes scoffed. 'Don't give me none of that. None of them lose a lick of sleep over your small spread. And they're all legit ranchers. They wouldn't risk hiring no one to do this and they got no reason.'

'You reckon it was Injuns? Comanche?'

asked Hicks from his horse.

Jim looked back at him, shook his head. 'No. Injuns would have taken the beef and they got too much respect for creatures. They only kill what they can use and they use near all of it.'

Jakes frowned. 'That don't leave us with many options, does it? Unless you got something to tell me.'

'It might be a one-time thing.' Jim said it too fast and he knew the foreman didn't believe a word of it.

'I can tell you don't believe that anymore than I do. You say you saw someone out in the field last night and the crazy old lady says she did too. That someone's most likely responsible for this here butchering. I got me a notion you know who that someone is.'

Jim shook his head, licked his lips. The flies buzzing about the dead cattle pricked his nerves and sweat trickling from beneath his arms irritated him.

'Only notion I might have ain't possible. Take my word for it.'

'Like to do that, Jim, but this has the

marks of a reckoning, for whatever reason.'

The sound of muffled hoof beats in the distance caught his attention and he looked up and back to see a man riding for them at a gallop.

'Things just got worse,' Jakes said, standing and peering at the approaching rider.

Jim straightened, glad to turn away from the sight of the dead cattle.

'Damn good beef gone to hell,' Hicks said, seemingly for no other reason than to ease some of the tension he was obviously feeling.

'That ain't the only thing likely to go to hell,' Jim said.

The rider came closer, his horse's hoofs pounding the grassy field in deliberate rhythm. Jim knew the rider well, worked for him part time, in fact.

'Wasn't your day to dep,' Jakes said. 'So reckon this ain't a social call.'

'No. It isn't.' Jim looked at Hicks. 'You inform him about the cattle?'

'No, sir, Mr Bartlett. Came straight

to you after I seen them.' The young man's tone was sincere and Jim knew he was telling the truth. That made the sinking sensation in his belly ten times worse because it meant trouble of some other kind and the notion that walls were suddenly closing in on him entered his mind.

You . . . can't . . . escape . . .

The rider pulled up, his tin star gleaming in the early morning sunlight. He paused, surveying the dead cattle with a sullen look, then shook his head.

'What the hell, Jim?' he asked.

'We were just asking our ownselves that, Marshal,' Jim said.

Marshal Tom Powers was a good man, resolute in his application of justice and absolute in his resistance to cowflap. A good twenty years Jim's senior, with thin balding hair and a face that looked as if pigeons had pranced across it, his blue eyes still held a twinkle of youth and his frame a firm command of presence. Jim knew the man to be fair, just and not easily deceived. He'd worked for him the past year and with each passing day had come to respect the lawdog all the more.

'Somebody got something out for you, Jim?' the marshal asked, then frowned. 'That's what it damn sure looks like.'

'Nobody I know should, least nobody living,' he said, a lack of conviction making the marshal eye him more seriously.

'Someone tell you about this?' Jakes asked the lawdog.

The marshal studied Jakes, the knowledge that the foreman had once been something other than what he was now plain on his face. He had expressed such to Jim a couple times, but after Jim had given Jakes his total support the lawman surrendered to Jim's judgment. Jim could tell the lawman still didn't completely trust the foreman, however.

'No, no one told me. This is as much a surprise to me as it probably is to you.

I rode out here about something unrelated — least I thought it was. The old woman told me she saw you ride over this way, so I came lookin'.' His gaze shifted back to Jim. 'Afraid this ain't the only bad news you're in for today, son.'

'What happened?' Jim asked, belly tightening more.

'You best come to town with me and see for yourself.'

Dread rose within him and his eyes widened. 'Emma?' His voice came high, almost pleading.

The lawman shook his head, leaned on the saddle horn. 'No, she's fine. Nothing to do with her. It's Billy . . . '

Weakness washed through Jim's legs and he leaned against his horse for support. Without the lawman even saying it Jim knew Billy was dead. He fought an urge to double over and vomit, everything around him going hazy. Heat flooded his face.

This isn't going to stop. . . .

'Son?' the marshal said.

'Huh?' he answered, only partially aware the lawman had spoken to him.

'You awright?' The marshal's gaze probed him, sympathetic yet questioning.

'Yes . . . yes.' He spat, let a curse slip from his lips, then climbed into the saddle. He glanced down at Jakes. 'You and Hicks get this and the others cleaned up.'

Jakes studied him. 'Anything else we should be on the lookout for?'

Jim knew what he meant but right now wasn't the time to discuss it.

'Reckon it pays to be on the alert after this.' With that, he reined around and gigged his horse into a ground-eating gait across the field, the marshal following suit. The day had barely begun but in Jim's estimation it already felt like it had gone on for a week. He reckoned what he would find in town would only make it feel all the longer.

★   ★   ★

'It ain't a pretty sight,' Marshal Powers said as they reined up in front of the general store. 'I'm tellin' you plain and I'm sorry about your friend.'

Jim nodded, swallowing hard and bracing himself for what he would see. He had ridden the entire way in silence, his mind racing through images of the past, settling on theories that should be impossible. Nobody had any reason to kill Billy Fredericks. Nobody except —

No. It can't be him.

'Billy was a good man, Marshal,' Jim said.

The lawdog nodded and swung down from the saddle. 'I know he was. I also know you two had a past of some sort together and were doing your best to put it behind you.'

Jim glanced at the older man. Powers was no fool. He'd likely figured out the story ages ago, if not the particulars. 'Men deserve second chances. I aimed to make the most of mine and so did Billy. Sometimes the past don't let that be, though. Sometimes some folks

44

won't let others repent.' He paused, stepped from the saddle. 'Same goes for Jakes. He's a good man, too.'

The marshal's face turned grim. 'I'm coming around on Jakes, but I've worked with you close enough to know what you say 'bout yourself and young Billy is the gospel. Some men . . . ' He shook his head, placed a boot on the steps leading to the boardwalk in front of the store. 'Some men can't change their nature. Certain types of men.' He peered harder at Jim.

'I ain't that type of man, neither is Jakes.'

The marshal nodded. 'Aware of that or I wouldn't have deputized you. But I ain't talking 'bout you or Jakes. I'm talking 'bout the other types, types a man such as yourself might have associated with at sometime in the past, types who would stop at nothing to get even. Those types don't change. They can't. And they got long memories.'

'I'll tell you what I told Jakes, Tom — it just ain't possible.'

45

'I got me a notion you don't totally believe that.'

Jim swallowed hard and went up the wooden steps to the boardwalk, ignoring the marshal's statement. Each bootfall on the old boards sounded unusually loud, reminding him of the thunder in his nightmare last night. Except now he realized what he had heard hadn't been thunder — it had been the sound of gunshots bleeding into his dream, gunshots that had killed his cattle.

He's back . . .

He went to the door, discovered it locked. The marshal came up beside him and pushed a key into the lock.

'Thought it best nobody got an early morning surprise with what, well, with what's inside. Gonna need you to be strong, boy, and do your duty as a deputy, too. We'll be needing to get the funeral man down here and inform some family, but I wanted you to see it first.'

'He didn't have no family.' Jim

stepped into the store. The bell chimed, mocking in its cheerfulness. Mid-morning gold arced through the window and fell across the aisles.

'Oh, Lord, no,' he muttered, stopping, his belly roiling at the sight of two old women sprawled on the floor. Bags of flour had burst around them, the result of bullets, he reckoned, and a dusty white powder covered the bodies that somehow made their death mask faces all the worse. Each had been shot, a single bullet from the looks of it. Canned goods that had tumbled from the shelves were scattered around them.

'The Twombly sisters,' the Marshal said. 'Unlucky enough to have come in extra early, I reckon.'

Jim fought down the bile surging into his throat. 'Billy sold them hooch. They didn't want the church ladies to know. Wasn't illegal, just . . . they were old.' He stood frozen, recollecting the sight of violent death from his past; it haunted the hell out of him.

'Whoever it was didn't come in here

to kill two old sisters, son,' the lawdog said. 'Had to be someone looking for Billy, for whatever reason.'

'Robbery?' He asked it without hope, already knowing the answer.

'Nothing appears to have been taken. I ain't got a list of all Billy's stock but if I was a betting man, I'd put my money on someone with a vendetta.'

Jim forced his legs to move. They shook, threatening to send him pitching to the floor, but he took a deep breath and regained some of his composure.

He went to the counter, saw Billy's outstretched hand, broken fragments of glass about him from shattered bottles. Liquor had stained the floor and its acrid aroma assailed his nostrils, but it wasn't the only repulsive scent. Another cloyed at his senses: bitter copper.

'He was shot, too,' the marshal said, pulling Jim from his thoughts. 'Once, in the head.'

Jim shuddered, then knelt beside the corpse. Emotion choked his throat and bile surged into his throat. For a moment the scene before him blurred with tears and he blinked until his vision cleared. The young man's eyes were wide with death, a round blue hole surrounded by dried brown blood gaping in his forehead.

'Near as I can tell only an hour or two ago. Whoever did it was kind enough to lock the front door from the inside, then go out the back.'

'Billy kept a spare key under — '

'The plant pot on the back porch.' The marshal nodded. 'I know; I used it to get in. Came over to pick something up on my way to the office and thought it was peculiar he wasn't open yet. He always opened right 'fore dawn. When I looked through the winder I saw the old ladies and let myself in the back.'

Jim kept staring at Billy's deathmask face, fighting the urge to vomit. 'Anyone see anything, who might have done it?'

'Somebody said they glimpsed a stranger in town but didn't get any kind of look at him. Might mean nothing.'

'Or everything . . . '

The marshal's brow lifted. 'You got a notion who this stranger might be?'

'A dead man.'

'What?'

Jim sighed and gently ran his hand over Billy's eyelids, closing them. 'He was like a brother to me, Tom. We went through a lot together, came out the other end.'

'I need a reason for his being dead, Jim. I know you got a suspicion. I can see it in your eyes.'

Unbidden anger spiked his innards. 'A reason? There ain't no reason for something like this.'

The marshal removed his hat, fingered the brim. 'You know what I mean.'

He knew. He knew damn well. But his mind would not let him accept that reason.

He straightened, holding back tears that threatened to spill. 'I want the man who done this. I want him to pay for this.'

Powers gave him an intense stare. 'Then maybe you got something to tell me?'

He shook his head, jaw muscles tightening. 'No . . . no, there's nothing.'

'I can damn well tell when someone's lying to me.' A note of irritation painted the lawdog's voice.

'It ain't so much a lie as an impossibility.'

'You said that before but there's three people dead in this store. Even if whoever you got a notion on ain't possible, I need to know.'

'Was this man, if somehow he is alive . . . It wouldn't make a lick of difference. It'd only get you killed.'

'You ain't being rational, boy.'

'Maybe I can't be right now.' He pushed past the lawdog and headed for the door. He needed to leave this room of death.

'Jim!' the marshal called behind him, but he ignored him, stepping out into the daylight and flinging the door shut behind him. He went to the rail, leaned over and vomited into the dust below.

A few folks on the street cast him a glance, probably thinking he was walking off a night of drunkenness, and went on about their business.

He dry-heaved for another moment, then finally got his nerves under control. He swiped a sleeve across his mouth and took deep breaths, then pushed himself away from the railing.

'Dammit, Billy!' he yelled, and slammed a fist against a support beam. 'Why'd you have to go and get yourself killed?' Tears welled again and the street blurred before him.

This shouldn't have been happening. It was impossible. He and Billy had created a new life, changed their ways. It wasn't goddamn fair! What kind of God gave them a second chance then suddenly took it away in the most horrible of manners?

Not God. No. Not His fault. That fault lay somewhere else, with a man spawned from the Devil's loins.

A dead man — a ghost.

It can't be. It simply can't be.

But dead cattle and dead folks didn't lie.

He lifted his hat and ran a hand through his hair, which was damp, his forehead moist with sweat.

He began to walk, trying to steady his legs. About him, the day seemed so mockingly serene, sunlight glittering from windows like stars and sparkling from troughs like diamonds. The warm breeze stirred tiny dust devils in the street. The scents of manure, smoked bacon from the café and sweet summer flowers mingled. A day like any other day.

Except his friend was dead, murdered, along with some of his cattle.

Serenity was relative. To those who strolled these boardwalks, nothing but a tranquil morning surrounded them. Peace. To him darkness swelled, an approaching storm, like the one in his nightmare.

No, that wasn't quite right, was it? No storm. Something — Someone else. Someone who had already arrived and was moving through the night and the day, leaving destruction and burning grief, and the promise of something so powerful and unrelenting Jim Bartlett could not stand against it.

'It . . . can't . . . be . . . him!' he said through gritted teeth.

'Jim!' a voice called out, snapping him from his thoughts and through bleary eyes he focused on a spot down the boardwalk. A young woman stood there, outside a dress shop. Her long brown hair cascaded free about her slender shoulders and she wore a simple gingham dress, blue, that hugged the curves of her body. She was a vision, enough to weaken a man's knees.

Emma Hanson. She owned the dress shop and was opening for the day's business.

She gave him an excited wave and started towards him. 'What are you doing in town so early?' she shouted to him, a smile like an angel's gracing her full lips.

He was about to answer when he stopped dead.

Someone stepped from an alley a dozen feet ahead of him, between him and Emma. A man, a man whose face he could not rightly see because the figure had pulled his battered hat low to cover his features in shadow. The man wore a gray duster and leaned against a building corner. A low laugh came from his lips.

'No . . . ' he muttered, heart thundering, everything around him becoming suddenly unreal, concave, as if he were looking through the wrong end of a spyglass.

The man looked up just a fraction and Jim caught a glimpse of something horrible beneath the hat.

Emma had stopped, a look of puzzled worry sweeping across her face and he knew she had witnessed the shocked expression on his features.

An instant later, the figure rolled backward around the corner into the alley. Jim remained frozen where he stood, staring at the empty place where the man had been.

4

Shaking off his spell, Jim bolted into motion a moment later. Had he truly even seen anyone standing there? Was his grief over Billy getting the better of him and somehow dredging up the figure from his nightmare?

Had Emma seen the man? Or was she merely reacting to his own stunned shock?

His boots thundered along the boardwalk as he ran for the alley. He wasn't thinking straight, wasn't contemplating that if the man he thought dead had indeed been standing there and was waiting for him in the alley, he would end up as dead as Billy.

Anger overrode any sense of caution and he leaped from the boardwalk to the ground in front of the alley. He had no gun, no way to defend himself against someone with a weapon.

But the alley was empty.

He started down it, shaking his head.

'Where are you?' he yelled, stopping, peering at the stacked crates and barrels lining either side of the alley. His eyes narrowed, picking out any spot a man might hide, but he saw no one. The alley led to a back street; Wendell was a latticelike affair of streets, with few twists and turns.

In motion again, he made his way to the other end of the alley and peered at the back street, studying each clapboard and brick building. The street appeared deserted. A breeze scooted a slip of telegraph paper across the dusty ground and fluttered a blanket hanging on a line outside a house.

But he saw no figure in a duster.

It was him . . .

It couldn't be!

A hand touched his shoulder and he started, whirled, hand closing into a fist. He stopped the fist an instant before he threw it, realizing it was Emma who had followed him, not the man he thought he'd seen.

'Judas Priest!' he said, a shudder working through him. He licked his lips, unable to move, his heart thudding in his throat.

'What's wrong, Jim?' Emma asked, concern in her brown eyes. No, not concern, entirely; something deeper. She had never seen him act this way and it frightened her. She had no notion of who or what he had been in the past, and he had no desire to tell her, but she glimpsed something in him she hadn't seen before.

'Did you see anyone . . . standing outside the alley?' he asked, afraid to hear her answer.

She shook her head, her eyes softening. 'No, but I wasn't looking. I was looking at you and I knew something was wrong. I saw you start running and came after you.'

He swung his head back around, glancing out at the back street a last time, then looked back to her.

Twenty minutes later found them at

the café. His hands shook as he clutched a cup of Arbuckle's. The heavy scents of beefsteak, eggs and coffee blended into a nauseating aroma and his belly roiled.

Emma cupped her hands about his. Her eyes turned sympathetic, yet still held a measure of worry. Maybe she thought he was loco. Hell, maybe he was. Maybe he had imagined that man.

'What's going on, Jim?' she asked. 'Please tell me. The way you're acting — this isn't you.'

You don't know who I am. . . .

He turned to the window and peered out into the street. The activity out there was starting to pick up as folks moved along the boardwalk, blissfully unaware of the darkness that had come to their town.

'Billy was killed this morning, in his shop,' he said. 'Murdered. The Twombly sisters with him.'

'Oh, my god.' Shock widened her eyes and deepened the lines of her young face. 'Did someone hold him up?'

'No.' He didn't elaborate, hoping she

59

wouldn't question him further, but he knew her too well to think that she would just let things go.

'Then what? Does the marshal have any idea who — '

'None!' he said, voice snapping out and he jerked his hands away from the cup and from beneath hers. He folded his arms across his chest, wondering if he could hold it together long enough to get back to the ranch.

'Jim, tell me what's wrong,' she said, startled by his harsh response, but her voice firm. She wasn't one to just back off, to let him get away with things.

'Nothing's wrong. He's just . . . ' He swallowed, trying to force back the emotion. 'He's just dead, all right? We'll find who did it and that will be that.'

She studied him for a dragging moment and he forced himself not to squirm under her gaze. She had this way about her that could probe into the depths of who a man was.

'What aren't you telling me?' she asked. 'There's more to it.' Her tone hardened. She wouldn't put up with him hiding things or lying to her. She'd had enough of that with her previous beau, she'd told him once, and she wasn't one to repeat her mistakes.

Truth to tell, he wasn't, either. That was why he felt the need to protect her from the ones he'd already made.

'Nothing else.'

'Jim . . . ' She drew out his name.

He searched his mind, looking for way to avoid saying anything that was a lie, yet too close to the truth.

'Some of my cattle, we found them dead this morning.'

'And by dead you don't mean they died of any disease.'

Sometimes she was too damn smart for her own good, he reckoned. 'No, someone killed them and left them there for me to find.'

'And you think it's the same someone who killed Billy.'

'Maybe,' he muttered, then took a sip of his coffee while he looked anywhere but in her eyes.

The café held a handful of tables covered with blue checked cloth, occupied by a few customers. He swallowed the coffee, its bitter taste not helping his nausea any.

'It isn't a maybe.' She touched his hand again and he resisted the urge to pull away. 'Tell me who it is. You saw a man and you looked like death had come calling on you.'

'I didn't see anyone. You didn't see him, so he wasn't there.'

She shook her head, dismissing his statement. 'He was there. I didn't see him but I didn't have to. I saw you and I saw your reaction. You saw someone you were afeared of, someone you know in some way. And that someone might be the reason your cattle and Billy died.'

'Just leave it be, Emma.' His voice came with a harsh command and he knew immediately she didn't cotton to it. She was too independent and would not put up with being spoken to in that manner. He reckoned in some ways she was tougher than any man in these parts and that came from standing up to them all her life. She raised herself pretty much alone, she had told him, after her parents were killed in a stage robbery. But, unlike him, she'd somehow gained strength from that event and chosen a path of her own, made herself an honest life.

'Don't speak to me that way, Jim.' Her tone said she was damn serious. 'I'm powerful sorry about your friend and about your cattle and I know you're grievin', so I'll let it pass this time. But don't take me for a fool. You might be able to convince your foreman or even the marshal there's no one stalking you but you won't convince me. I know you too well.'

Do you? Do you really, Emma?

He pulled his hand away again, anger rising, despite himself. He was in no mood for this and no matter how much he loved her he refused to bring his past down on her.

It will come down on her anyway.

You're just being yellow, running from the truth . . .

Balls of muscle knotted to either side of his jaw as he clenched his teeth. He stood, reached into a pocket, brought out a greenback, then tossed it on to the table.

'Jim,' Emma said, starting to rise. 'Please don't shut me out.'

'You ain't entitled to everything about me,' he said, his voice crueler than he recollected hearing it having been for the past two years. It was something left over from the old days and he despised it and knew it hurt her, though anger flared in her eyes.

'What *am* I entitled to, then? Waiting forever for you to make up your mind and decide whether you love me or not? Waiting for you to let the ghosts haunting you free and to trust me enough with them?'

'That's not what I meant.'

'Really?' Her eyes narrowed. 'I'm not a toy, Jim. I'm not there to take out when you want to play with me, then discard the moment you think you're getting too attached. Like I said, I'll let it pass because you're grievin' — '

'You do that, Emma. You let it pass. It'll be a hell of a lot safer for you that way.'

'You're crazy if you think that. Whatever this is, whatever or whoever's come for you, he'll know I'm part of your life, and if I don't know what's comin' I won't have any chance to fight it.'

'It's my fight.'

'It's *our* fight.'

'No.' He spun, stalked towards the door. He knew she was watching him go, making no effort to follow, despite the anger and hurt welling in her being. She would chase no man. Either that man wanted to be with her or leave; it was his choice. She wasn't about to beg or saddle him. That was just her.

He stepped out on to the boardwalk, his belly churning again and his heart full of pain, grief, fear. In the space of twenty-four hours his life was being turned upside down, a life he'd spent two years building. Maybe it had never been real. Maybe who he was was who he had been. Would always be. Maybe you couldn't escape the past after all.

*   *   *

After leaving the café, Jim spent most of the day helping the marshal make arrangements for Billy's funeral, as well as informing the sisters' next of kin about their deaths. He'd made a cursory search of the town, but discovered no trace of the man in the duster; the figure might as well have been a ghost and the more he thought about it the more he doubted his own sanity. Upon questioning some of the townsfolk, he found no one else had seen such a man, either.

He sat at the dining room table, a plate of beefsteak, fried potatoes and greens before him. His belly and nerves in turmoil, he had no desire to eat. He'd subsisted on coffee all day, but he reckoned he best force himself to put something down because of what was coming . . .

What was coming was worse than what had already been. Though it should have been impossible, a man was here — a man from the past. Stalking him, trying to dismantle the new life he'd built. He wasn't crazy. He *had* seen that man —

You saw a man. It might not be him.

He wished he could convince himself that that was the case. But he'd been thinking on it all day, and with each moment the possibility became greater in his mind. How? How could that man have escaped his fate? It wasn't possible.

It was.

Dammit!

He banged a fist against the table, the plate jumping and coffee splashing over the edge of his cup. This was no figment of a nightmare, or grief. He had seen that figure, and cattle and people were dead.

And if it wasn't . . . that man, then who? Someone who knew about the past? Someone who had worked for —

A twinge of dread interrupted his thoughts: Emma. If whoever it was had seen her, connected them, way she said . . .

'You gonna eat that or just threaten to beat it to death?' a voice came, tearing him from his reverie.

'What?' he mumbled, blinking.

'You ain't said a word all evening,' came Jakes's voice from the end of the table, shaking Jim from his thoughts. The foreman was peering at him with a probing look. 'Then you pound the table. You got something on your mind?'

'Reckon nothing I want to share.' He picked up his fork, stabbed a piece of beefsteak, then shoved it into his mouth. The meat tasted flavorless, and a poor choice for a meal after seeing his murdered cattle earlier in the day.

Jakes uttered a small laugh. 'I reckon there's lots you need to share. And it's about time you did.'

'It's my problem, I'll handle it,' he insisted, chewing the meat and swallowing it. He washed it down with a gulp of coffee, hoping the foreman would let it drop.

'Reckon it's your past but not just your problem. Least not anymore.' Jakes paused and looked towards the kitchen to make sure the old woman wasn't within listening range. 'Look, Jim, whoever this fella is that's come after you — '

'Don't know there is one. I might have imagined him last night.' His words came too fast and held no conviction; at this point he was simply trying to deny the obvious, to his foreman and to himself.

Jakes frowned. 'And the old woman imagined him, too, and you imagined him in town today?'

'How'd you — '

'Saw Miss Emma when I went into Wendell for supplies.'

Anger flared in his being, and his grip

tightened on his fork. He stabbed another piece of meat. 'She shouldn't have said anything.'

'She's worried about you. We all are. She said you saw this fellow there, in town. And no ghost killed Billy or those cattle.'

'You get them cleaned up?' He hoped changing the subject would take the foreman off the trail he was riding.

Jakes nodded and took a sip of his coffee. The ranch hand, Hicks, had already eaten and left to go to the saloon.

'Son, this problem belongs to everyone here on the ranch now. Me, Hicks, even that old woman.'

'And Emma . . . ' he muttered.

Jakes nodded again. 'And Emma. And if you don't come out with it we got no way of knowing what's coming or what to look out for. No way to protect ourselves.'

'He wants me, not you.'

Jakes offered a scoffing grunt. 'He wants you but he'll go through everyone around you to reach his end, whatever that end is. I'm assuming he wants a reckoning for something, whoever this fella might be. That type don't care who they hurt to reach their goal. You think your friend will be his last kill?'

'Billy and me, we . . . we were associated. That's why he killed him. He's got no reason to come after anyone else. He wants me.'

'Even if that's true you best have me or Hicks or the marshal with you wherever you go from now — '

'No!' Jim slammed a fist on the table again. 'I won't be looked after like some helpless calf. I don't need protecting.'

Jakes frowned. 'No, you don't. You need friends. You need someone to get your back.'

He dropped his fork on the plate and put his face in his hands. Jakes was right, dammit, but stubborn pride and fear were getting in the way. He didn't want the man to know who he had been, didn't want to lose his respect, despite the fact the man himself had a questionable past.

Moments later, his face lifted out of his hands. 'I can't, Jakes. I have to handle this man myself, if it is this man. You don't know what he is. I got lucky two years ago. I know it and if he's alive and there's no damn way he should be, he knows it. That's why he's here taking me apart piece by piece. He didn't need Billy because Billy wasn't the one who . . . '

'Who what?' Jakes asked, his eyes intense.

'Who killed him.'

Jakes nodded, a measure of comprehension coming to his features. 'Reckon I understand. You killed a man. It's been tearing your gut apart. But I reckon this man was someone who needed killing. I've run into types such as that in my own travels. Some men are just plain evil and need to be put down 'fore they can hurt others.'

'He did hurt others. But there's more to it than just that. This man — You're right, he needed killing. More than any man ever did.'

'Then tell me the rest. Tell me who he is.'

Jim's gaze rose to the window, peered out into the night.

'That man is dead.'

'Plain to see he ain't. And your stubbornness is gonna get you killed. You need friends, Jim.'

'I had one and he's dead. Reckon my friendship gets folks killed, not my stubbornness.'

'So what do you do, then? Ride out alone all the time hoping he'll come after you and leave everyone else alone? Isolate those from your life you reckon he might use against you?'

'I . . . ' He hesitated, emotion choking his throat. 'I don't know.'

'Then you best figure it out because I'm wagering this man ain't gonna give you a lot of time. Go to the marshal if you won't let me help. Tell him what you were and who this man is.'

Jim shook his head. 'I can't. He

wouldn't understand and he's as likely to throw me in a cell as him.'

Jakes sighed a heavy sigh. 'I right doubt it. He knows you as well as anyone. Treats you like a son more than a deputy. And as much as I think he distrusts me, he ain't stupid. He's figured you out, least part of the ways. If he wanted you in a cell you would be there by now.'

'Ain't his worry.'

'Ain't it? He's got a man and two old women shot to death in the general store. Town's gonna want to know who did it and want justice. Can you give them that? Or you just plan on giving them more bodies to bury?'

Jim never got a chance to answer. From the kitchen came a short scream, then the shattering of a plate.

5

Jim launched from his chair as if stage springs had let go. His heart jumped into his throat as he bolted for the kitchen, Jakes a half step behind him.

The kitchen was small; pots and pans hung from a rack above a small center counter and the cast iron stove occupied the south corner. Mrs Pendergast stood near the counter, gazing out into the deepening night through a window above the sink. About her feet lay shards of a plate she had dropped.

'What happened?' Jim asked, trying to get his heart to settle back into his chest.

'The Devil . . . ' the old woman said, her gaze not wavering from the window.

'What the hell are you talkin' about, old woman?' Jakes said, the foreman's patience obviously strained.

'The Devil . . . ' the old woman

repeated. 'He was out there, just standing there, lookin' into the house.'

'What'd this Devil look like?' Jim asked, his belly dropping.

'Was wearin' a long coat, he was, had a hat pulled so low I couldn't see his face but I know he was evil, Mr Bartlett. I know he was.' The old woman shuddered as if her bones would shake apart.

'And how'd you know that?' Jakes said, frowning and going to the window to look out.

'I could feel it,' the old woman said. 'Like the fella brought the night with him.'

'You're plumb loco, you know that?' Jakes said. 'He was just a man.'

Jim wasn't entirely sure the old woman wasn't right. This man — if he was alive — was indeed as close to the Devil as any man could come.

But he wouldn't let that stop him. If this man wanted a confrontation he would get one. He whirled and went back through the dining room to the parlor. He grabbed a Winchester from pegs mounted on the wall above the fireplace, then levered a shell into the chamber.

By the time he returned to the kitchen, Jakes had unholstered his Colt and was checking the chambers. He gazed at Jim.

'Stay inside,' Jim told the old woman.

She nodded. 'I ain't about to go out there.' She went to the hanging pot rack and grabbed a cast-iron skillet, clutching it in bony white hands.

'Let me go first.' Jim moved past Jakes to the door, pulled it open and stepped out into the darkness.

Long shadows swayed across the ground, stretching from the corral and barn, outbuildings and scattered cottonwood stands. Moonlight glazed leaves and grass and sliced across the grounds in razorlike wedges.

Somewhere a night bird uttered a peculiar warbling sound.

'You see anything?' Jakes asked, coming up behind him, eyes narrowed.

He surveyed the grounds, noting the bunkhouse was dark with Hicks in town.

'Nothing.'

'Only so many places a fella could hide,' Jakes said.

Jim nodded. 'Trees.' He ducked his chin out at the field.

'Behind one of the buildings,' Jakes said.

'Barn,' Jim added. They both looked in the direction of the barn and his nerves buzzed. Muscles tightened to either side of his jaw.

'Door's open . . . ' Jakes said.

Jim's belly cinched. He started towards the barn. As he approached, he slowed, angled towards the side and kept against the wall. Jakes followed suit.

'The horses are shuffling, making noises,' Jakes said.

'We would have heard gunshots if he did to them what he did to the cattle. Reckon his aim wasn't that this time.'

'Maybe his aim was just to be seen

and that's why he let that old woman catch a glimpse of him.'

'But why?'

Jakes shrugged. ''Cause he wants you to know he's watching, waiting. He wants you to know — '

He's coming, Jim completed in his mind.

He eased along the side of the barn to the front corner and peered around. He saw nothing except one of the big doors standing open. He hadn't left it that way.

'If he's in there . . . ' Jakes said.

'He's likely armed.'

Jakes nodded, lifting his Colt to his chest. Jim's hands tightened about the Winchester's stock and barrel and he swung around the corner, sidled up to the open door and chanced a look inside.

Pitch blackness swarmed within the barn. Moonlight penetrated through the hayloft window but not to the lower level. The scent of manure and hay and horse urine blended into a sharp musk that assailed his nostrils. Normally he found that odor pleasant, reassuring, in a way, of the new life he had created for himself. But now it only tightened his nerves and warned him that that life could be taken away in an instant.

'See anything?' Jakes whispered.

Jim shook his head. 'Too goddamn dark.'

'Then we best face it.' Jakes suddenly moved around him and stepped into the opening.

'Dammit,' Jim said under his breath, unable to halt the foreman in time; Jakes did not know the caliber of the man he was dealing with. In a single panic-filled moment, he expected to hear the blast of a gun and lose another friend.

But no shot came.

Jim moved into the barn behind Jakes, senses alert, the hair on the back of his neck prickling.

'What the hell you think you're doing?' he said to the foreman in a stabbing whisper.

'This fella wanted to openly take a shot he'd have ambushed you right out of the house. Got a feeling he's got something else in mind.'

'Your feeling was wrong, you'd have swallowed a bullet.'

Jakes glanced back at him and now that Jim's eyes were adjusting somewhat to the darkness he could see an annoyed expression on the man's face.

'Then you best tell me who we're dealing with here.'

'Who *I'm* dealing with. Ain't your problem.'

'Beg to differ.' The foreman moved deeper into the barn and Jim followed, his grip tightening on the rifle until his hands and forearms ached. His head swiveled, his gaze picking out the outlines of horses in their stalls. One of them nickered, bobbing his head and another shuffled his feet.

'There's no one in here,' Jakes said. 'Horses are too calm. They'd be more riled at a stranger. These beasts are right particular and damn near as loco as that old woman you got in your house.'

Jim nodded, knowing the foreman was right. Whoever had been out here was gone now. The man had only wanted to alert them that he was watching, as Jakes had said.

Watching or . . .

'Oh, God, no — ' Jim blurted and whirled.

'What's wrong?' Jakes said, voice startled, bolting into motion a beat behind the young rancher.

Jim was already moving through the barn door. 'A distraction, Jakes,' he yelled back over his shoulder. 'I should have known. He used to work that way back in Colorado. Send Billy in first sometimes to — '

'What the hell are you talking about?' Jakes blurted.

Ignoring the query, Jim ran for the house. His heart had leaped into his throat and sweat sprang out on his forehead. Panic thundered through his mind: he had made a mistake. It had been too long, his judgment of the man now rusty, unable to predict his moves the way he had been capable of doing when they'd worked together two years ago.

'No, no, no . . . ' he mouthed, tears coming to his eyes. He knew, he *knew* he was too late. Distraction. Misdirection. For all that man had been he had been nothing if not a tactician, a magician of sorts. It had saved him from a hangman's noose countless times. Only happenstance had brought about his death.

Jim charged into the kitchen. Images flashed through his mind as he stopped just inside the door, images of the past two years and of the old woman's irascible ways and often foolish talk.

Feeling sorry for her, he had hired her after her husband died, though she was obviously not riding with a full saddle. She had become a surrogate grandmother of sorts, replacing those he had never known and he had come to love her as such.

And now it was over.

An agonized scream tore from his throat. He couldn't have stopped it had he wanted to.

She hung there, a rope thrown over a ceiling rafter, its noose end taut about her thin neck. The frying pan lay on the floor, as if it were a mocking symbol that nothing could protect anyone against this man.

'No!' he swung the rifle back and forth, but the room was empty except for the hanging woman. He tossed the rifle to the counter, grabbed a butcher's knife from a block and ran to her. He lifted her frail form in a desperate hope that somehow he was in time, that her heart still beat and her lungs still breathed. He sliced through the rope and gently lowered her to the kitchen floor, falling to his knees beside her. He pried the rope from about her neck but he knew it was too late: her bulging eyes told him as much.

He pulled her to his chest; she felt like a frail bird that had slammed into a window. Tears streamed from his eyes.

'Judas Priest . . . ' came Jakes's voice behind him and Jim looked up and back with pleading, grief-filled eyes.

'He wanted us out there chasing ghosts,' he said. 'He wanted us to leave the house long enough for him to do this.'

Jakes nodded, his Adam's apple bobbing. 'This man . . . he's some kind of monster.'

'The Devil, way she said. He's the goddamned Devil.'

★ ★ ★

Jim lay on his bed in the darkness, staring up at the moonlight-dappled ceiling. All emotion seemed to have leached from his soul, at least for the moment.

He recollected times in the past when the old woman had scolded him, always with a grandmotherly glint in her eye. He recalled the times he had laughed it off, only to be scolded some more and lectured on respecting his elders.

He missed her, powerfully, and it was his fault she was dead. If he had told Jakes . . .

No, it wouldn't have mattered. They would have still gone out after that man, still been led away because in the last two years Jim Bartlett had gone soft. He was no longer that hard man from his past; he had become what he wanted to become — a legitimate rancher struggling to atone for a life that never should have been.

And now she was gone. Billy, too. Who would be next? Jakes? Hicks? Emma?

Without realizing it, he drifted off, grief washing over him in cascading waves as he sank into a fitful slumber.

Thunder. From the night. Boom, boom, boom. A storm of blackness, a storm of the soul. Lightning sizzled across a bloated black sky and he stood in the field again, a raging sense of loss overwhelming him. He saw her, the old woman, her dark skeletal form swaying from a cottonwood branch, her damning glassy eyes accusing him of what he knew to be true: he had caused her death as surely as if he had taken the rope and strung her up himself.

'Nooo!' he shouted and the thunder boomed again and blood rained from the sky —

Jim sat bolt upright in bed, breath beating out, heart slamming, sweat streaming down his face and chest.

You cannot escape . . .

'Oh, God . . . ' he muttered, burying his face in his hands, tears flowing again and the powerful sense of loss rushing through him in shuddering waves. After long moments of sobbing, he swung his feet out of bed. His boots hit the floor with a thunder of sound that jolted him.

The marshal had come out, questioned them about the man they had seen and Jakes had given the lawdog as much detail as there was, which wasn't a hell of a lot. Powers had asked Jim a few questions but hadn't pressed the issue because of his loss, but the time would come when he would want answers. The lawdog had searched the grounds with Jakes but had come up empty. Meanwhile, Jim had dealt with the funeral man, the old woman's body on a sofa, covered with an afghan she had crocheted and kept wrapped about her shoulders constantly in the winter months.

He stood, went to the French doors, opened them and stepped out on to the balcony.

Night air blowing against his face caused a chilled evaporation of tears.

He went to the railing, for a moment afraid he would see her body hanging from a cottonwood.

But he saw something else: a figure, bathed in shadow and cold moonlight, duster swaying in the breeze.

He whirled, plunged through the doors and across the room. He took the stairs in leaps and ran to the parlor. After grabbing the Winchester, he dashed to the front door, throwing it open. In heartbeats, he was across the veranda and running across the field towards where he had seen the figure.

But the figure had disappeared. As fast as he had made it down the stairs and out the door, the ghostly form in the duster had been faster, vanishing into the night.

He swung the rifle back and forth, finger jammed into the trigger guard, heart banging.

'Where are you, you bastard?' he yelled. 'Come and get me now! Coward!'

He listened, swore he caught the faint echo of a laugh on the breeze. A laugh from the past.

6

The boy was hiding something, thought Marshal Tom Powers as he poured coffee from a blue enameled pot into a tin cup. He took a sip, grimaced.

'Damn,' he muttered. 'I gotta get me a woman. Still can't make coffee that tastes like anything but horse piss.'

He turned away from the small table and went to the chair behind his desk. Lowering himself into the chair, he sighed, then set the cup on the desktop. The office was small, the bank of three cells to the back unoccupied. It was a rare day when they held a tenant and even then it was usually someone sleeping off a drunk. This was a peaceful town and folks weren't inclined to get rowdy much, despite the cattle ranches in the area and the cowboys who came into town to let off steam.

At least it *had* been a peaceful town.

In a bit over twenty-four hours he had four killings on his hands, more than he recalled having in all his years as marshal.

Someone had come to this town, someone cruel and evil. And he had a powerful notion that boy knew who that someone was.

Yesterday, he'd spent the day checking about the town for someone who might have seen anyone in the vicinity of the general store near the time Billy Fredericks and the sisters were murdered, but had come up empty. One person thought they had seen a stranger dressed in a duster, but hadn't gotten a look at the man's face, so it might have been someone from town. Impossible to tell, the witness had said.

But a stranger would have to be camping somewhere close, yet nowhere obvious in town, where he was likely to be noticed. A quick check of the boarding houses and hotel had determined no one new had rented a room.

Powers recalled the outlying arroyo

held any number of small caves. A man could camp there and not be seen, he reckoned. Perhaps later he'd ride on out that way and check around. Yet, even if a stranger were there, finding him would be like finding a needle in a haystack. Worse, because this stranger wanted to remain unseen, he had a knack for slipping around unnoticed and committing crimes without witnesses. He also had a bead on that boy, and likely the folks close to Jim Bartlett. Perhaps he was even an old lawdog himself.

His gaze rose to the window as sunlight streamed through in dusty arcs and fell across the worn floorboards. It might just have been another ordinary day if not for all the death that had descended upon this town. Last night, another murder, the old woman who worked for Jim Bartlett. He'd known her in passing but he had seen the look of utter grief on the boy's face. Whoever was stalking young Bartlett knew how to hurt him. Powers saw a method to this killer's madness: it was a personal vendetta, not a power grab for the ranch, despite the dead cattle. That meant the boy knew the killer from somewhere in his past.

He had an idea who that man might be, but like the boy had alluded to, it should have been impossible.

The marshal swung around in his chair, took a sip of his coffee, then leaned over and slid open a bottom drawer. He drew out three large pieces of paper and tossed them on to his desk. With a sigh, he sifted through them for the third time since yesterday morning.

His gaze focused on one dodger in particular, that of a man two years missing, presumed dead.

He stared at the hard face on the paper, coldness pricking his nerves, a chill waving through the small hairs on the back of his neck.

'Are you a ghost?' he muttered, despite the fact he had never believed in such things. The outlaw had terrorized

Colorado Territory a couple years back, then vanished. He shuffled the dodger aside, scanned the two beneath it.

Jim Bartlett would be shocked to learn Powers had known all along who he was hiring as a deputy, and who ran the general store. The kid had never said a word about his past and it was clear he was trying to outrun it, start over, but Powers would have been a damn poor lawdog not to have realized something was odd about the way those two had just appeared in Wendell and bought a ranch and store.

He'd watched them for a spell, then discovered the dodgers on them and this third man with whom they'd once ridden. At first, he had puzzled over the fact that wanted men would settle in this nowhere town. Were they the first in a wave of something bigger? Or were they men trying to reclaim their morality?

As the months passed and no outlaw invasion occurred, he had settled on his second notion: second chances. It came down to second chances. Those men had escaped a life they had either chosen or been trapped in and were seeking to make things right. He'd seen them do charitable work. That's why he had offered the young man the deputy job, not only to keep him close but to see to it that second chance worked out. He could have taken them in, he reckoned, but something about them told him they had been two men caught up in events too big for them to handle. Would throwing them in a cell have done any good? Righted the wrongs any more than the effort they were making?

Depends on who you asked, he reckoned. Some unforgiving types would say no and claim he was falling down on his duty by not arresting them both. But he saw something in those two that told him they would do far more good in the long run with the penance they set for themselves than any cell or a hangman's noose could to help restore what had already been done.

Over time, he had been proven right.

Billy had given poor folks credit and supplies they could not afford when times got tough. And young Bartlett, he attended church every Sunday, provided free beef for some families hit hard by sickness or poverty, and contributed more to the community than any single individual. Whatever they had done in the past, well, he reckoned they had made up for it.

The Lord forgave, and so did Marshal Powers.

But the past didn't want to let them alone. This man they had escaped, he was supposed dead. Marshal Powers had checked into it and not a sighting of this outlaw had occurred within the past two years. He had simply vanished, as though he had stepped off the face of the earth.

But more than that, he felt certain Jim Bartlett had inside knowledge the man was dead. Perhaps he and young Billy had even somehow brought about that demise; if they had, they had done the world a favor. This man — he took the first dodger and placed it atop the others — this man was a cold-blooded butcher.

But what if they hadn't killed him? What if that man in the duster the witness glimpsed had been him?

Why wait two years to return? the marshal asked himself. Why now?

'Because Jim now had a new life and everything to lose,' he muttered. And maybe it had taken time to find the boy. After all, the names had been changed, both Jim's and Billy's.

'Judas H. Priest, I wish you'd talk to me,' the marshal said. He wagered young Bartlett likely had some fool notion about handling it himself, perhaps the way he had handled his escape in the first place.

But this man . . . The marshal tapped the top dodger, staring at it. This man was too deadly for the boy to handle on his own. Fact, he was even too deadly for a small-town marshal. Powers would telegraph the county authorities later today with his suspicions and fetch help before anyone else ended up looking at the wrong side of a pine box.

A sound roused him from his thoughts, the scuffing of a boot, and his gaze jerked from the wanted dodger to a man who seemed to have materialized suddenly in front of his desk.

'How'd — ' he started, then noticed the back door hung open.

'Took me the liberty of prying the lock last night while you weren't here, Marshal,' the man said, his voice low, cold. He wore a gray duster and a low-pulled hat that shadowed his face. An arc of sunlight backlit him, adding to the effect that some devil had appeared before him, and a chill crawled down his spine.

'Who are you?' he asked, already knowing the answer, but standing his ground. He had never backed down to any man nor beast and he refused to start now.

'Reckon you know who I am.' The man made a gesture with his left hand index finger towards the dodger on the marshal's desk. 'Not a very good likeness, is it? Least not anymore.'

The man lifted his head, allowing the lawdog a look at the face beneath.

'Christ on a crutch ... ' he whispered, for the first time a measure of fear taking hold.

'Death changes a man, Marshal.' The man didn't move.

The marshal started to go for the gun at his hip, but his hand stopped in mid-motion as the stranger's own hand swept free of the duster, a Smith & Wesson gripped in a scarred fist.

'I've been watching him a long time, Marshal. I know he works for you and I know any lawdog worth his salt would have figured out who he was by now. I also figured when bodies started piling up you'd find the trail led back to me fast enough. Still posters out on us, as you're well aware.'

'He's changed,' the marshal said. 'He ain't like your kind anymore. Leave him be.'

'See, I can't do that.' The man

hesitated, his head lifting a bit higher, giving the marshal a better look. The lawdog fought the urge to recoil.

'He not only took my life but where do you think he got all that money to start over?'

'He's doing good with that money, atoning for his sins.'

The man uttered a low laugh. 'No one atones for sin. Sin creeps into your soul like boll weevils infesting cotton, Marshal. Sin never goes away, it only waits, till the day it can come back stronger than ever before.'

The marshal's gaze didn't waver. 'Death turned you into some kind of bad philosopher?' Powers contemplated his options, which took all of a second because he had none. This man wasn't going to leave him alive and he knew it. His only choice was a desperate move.

'Death turned me into a monster.'

'You were already a monster — '
Powers went for his gun.

He never made it. The sound of thunder crashed through the small office and burning pain punched into his chest. He slammed back into his chair and gazed down to see a crimson orchid blooming on his chest. As blackness swelled from the corners of his mind, he said a silent prayer the boy would survive and send this monster into death a final time.

* * *

Jim reined to a halt at the edge of his property as the sun slipped deeper into the western horizon. His gaze swept across the grassy plains to the western arroyo. Nothing. He'd found nothing, except some flattened grass where possibly a man might have been standing last night. But no hoof marks that would have left a trail to where that man might have gone.

He reckoned there weren't many places a man could hide out here in the open fields, unless it was in one of the arroyo caves, but he'd spent half the day searching that area for any signs of a squatter, only to come up empty. He supposed some of that search had been with the idea of purposely making himself a target, challenging the man, but it had not worked.

The man was stalking him, playing by his own rules, and nothing Jim could do would draw him out of his game plan.

You have to tell Jakes . . .

The thought had ridden through his mind a number of times over the past couple of hours, along with arguments against such an action. He had nearly convinced himself the man would only come for him after killing Billy, but now he knew that wasn't true, had never been; this man would come after everyone he cared about before he finally revealed himself. He had to tell the foreman everything; he couldn't risk letting Jakes get caught off guard the way the old woman had been. Telling Jakes might not have saved her in the long run, but at least the foreman was good with a gun.

That left Emma. If the man had been watching him long enough, and Jim felt sure he had, then Emma was a target. And he couldn't let anything happen to her.

After swinging around, he gigged his horse into a ground-eating gait across the field in the direction of town.

He would not tell her about the man, the way he planned to do with Jakes; he would not reveal his past, not yet, not until it ended with either the man's death or his own.

The man's death. Hadn't he already killed him? How many times did a man have to die before he stayed dead?

He's inhuman . . .

No, he was just a man, a vile man, and somehow something had gone wrong that day.

His thoughts turned back to the young woman and something in his heart clutched. What he had to do was perhaps more difficult than his choice to go straight two years ago. Because it would mean hurting her, perhaps even destroying any chance for his own happiness should he survive the coming days. He owed her more than hurt, but what other choice was there? He could not risk her life.

His hands tightened on the reins and he drew deep breaths, telling himself he was making the right decision.

He had no choice. No choice at all.

He reached town a few moments later and slowed the bay to a fast walk. The sun had dipped further and dusky shadows stretched from buildings. His gaze scanned the street, searching in a vain hope for any sign of the devil he knew must be lurking.

But he saw nothing. Folks walked about, giving him little notice. They had seen him in town often enough. He angled his horse towards the small dress shop on a corner near the gunshop and mercantile.

After he reined up, he slipped from the saddle, legs unsteady as he hit the ground, heart suddenly banging.

'Deputy Bartlett?' came a voice and

he turned to see an older woman on the boardwalk hurrying towards him, a pie in her brown-spotted thick hands.

'Miss Gulliver,' he said, tipping a finger to his hat.

The woman rushed up to him, her face red, and gave him a smile. The heavy scent of some flowery perfume hit his nostrils and he noted she was wearing her Sunday best, a high-collared dress. Her well-rounded figure stretched the flower-print fabric to its limit.

'You haven't seen Marshal Powers, have you?'

'No, not today, ma'am.'

'I baked him this cherry pie but his office was locked. I haven't seen him all day.'

Jim knew the woman had a thing for the marshal, though the marshal wasn't returning the emotion at this juncture. 'Haven't seen him. Reckon he's been out searching.'

'Searching for what, Deputy? Lordy, I swear, that man works too much.'

Searching for a dead man, he wanted to say but didn't. 'Reckon for the store owner's killer.'

She nodded like a chubby jackrabbit. 'Oh my, yes, I heard tell something terrible happened. Imagine, in a peaceful town like Wendell. Whatever is the world coming to, Deputy?'

'Wish to hell I knew, Miss Gulliver. Wish to hell I knew.' He left her standing there holding her pie and went into the dress shop.

The moment he entered, his heart started pounding again and he took a deep breath. This was harder than he expected, his feelings for Emma deeper. He was a fool not asking for her hand ages ago. And now that option might never be.

She stood behind the counter towards the rear of the store and looked up as the bell above the door chimed upon his entrance. A tentative smile came to her full lips.

He angled along the aisles of dresses and ladies' apparel, his mind focused on one thing, saying what he had come to say.

'I'm sorry,' she said as he reached the counter. 'I shouldn't have been so hard on you yesterday. You had just lost your friend and now I heard Mrs Pendergast — '

He nodded, licked his lips, swallowed at the emotion balling in his throat. For a moment he was unable to speak.

She came around the counter and gently touched his arm. 'Let me help you, Jim. Tell me what's happening.'

He wanted to turn away, walk on out of the store and relinquish the duty he'd fostered upon himself. But that would only get her killed too, wouldn't it?

'I'm sorry, Emma,' he said, almost a whisper. 'I came to tell you something and I hope you won't hate me.'

'What is it?' Her face changed, then, and he knew she glimpsed his resolve in his eyes. Her eyes narrowed and hardness washed into them.

'I can't see you anymore.' He blurted

it before he had the chance to change his mind.

Shock hit her face, though he was certain she had sensed the words coming. 'What? Why? What's going on, Jim? Whatever it is we can — '

'No, dammit! I want you out of my life. Go away from here for a while. Don't ever talk to me on the street again if you see me.' His words trembled and though tears flooded his eyes he held them back.

'What's going on?' she demanded, defiance and anger coming with her tone. 'This isn't you. You wouldn't throw away everything we have. I know better.'

He jerked his arm away, lashed out at a rack holding dresses and knocked it over. It landed with a loud clatter, garments flying off. He looked at her. 'You don't know me at all. You don't know what I was and what I was was a bastard. I'm still that man, Emma, and that man don't want you in his life.'

She stared at him, for one of the few times he could recollect, speechless and hurt beyond anything he had expected.

'Please . . . ' she said, the first time he had ever heard her plead for anything.

'Get the hell out of my life,' he said, his voice as harsh as he could make it. He whirled, stormed from the store, leaving her staring at his back. Everything inside him wanted to come apart and he barely made it out of the place before tears came from his eyes. His legs threatened to go out from beneath him. He went to his horse, pulled himself into the saddle, nearly slipping right back off. He had done what needed doing, he told himself. No more death could result from his past mistakes. He had not had any choice and now she would be safe.

He took deep breaths, noticing her face in the window, looking out at him, tears rolling down her cheeks, and he almost climbed back off his horse and went to her. It took every ounce of his strength to stop himself from doing so. He reined around, headed out into the street.

Doing the right thing sometimes caused the most anguish, he thought, not daring to look back and see her face again. Maybe he should not have done the right thing two years ago. Maybe he should have simply acquiesced to the dark life he had once lived and he would have been hanging from a cottonwood by now.

Choices. Never easy ones, but necessary ones that tore him in pieces and made him half wish the man stalking him would put a bullet in his back right that very moment.

* ★ ★

The man leaned on the corner of the building a street down from the dress shop, staying just out of sight of the Bartlett boy as he came out of the dress shop. Something had happened between them, that boy and the young woman who owned the store.

Oh, he had watched the boy long enough to know that he had something for the young woman, something powerful, and now the boy was trying to prevent something from happening to her. But he could not. It was too late.

'You don't have the skill to best me,' the man whispered. 'You never did. You got lucky but your luck's run out.'

Things were going right well, he assured himself, pleased. That boy was coming apart. It wouldn't take much more, but there was still a lot of heartache and death to come.

The man laughed, that laugh hanging in the air like a living thing. Then he faded back into the alley, merging with the encroaching shadows, satisfied beyond measure with his deeds and eager for the terror yet to come.

7

A cloud of Durham smoke hung in the air and strident giggles from sateen-bodiced saloon gals punctuated the shouts and curses of cowboys. The women leaned over the shoulders of men playing Faro and poker, hoping to share in their winnings, whispering silky promises of pleasure into their ears. The clanking of an out-of-tune tinkler jangled through the barroom.

Jim Bartlett turned his back to it all, hunched over the bar, a whiskey bottle in front of him. The barkeep, wiping out a glass, cast him an occasional bemused gaze, unused to him being in here at all, and Jim couldn't blame him. The drawn look on his face he saw staring back at him from the spider-veined, gild-framed mirror behind the bar portrayed a weary sight, that's for sure. Dark half-circles nested beneath his red-webbed eyes and he looked as if he had aged ten years over night.

Maybe he had. And maybe it didn't matter any longer. He had already lost a friend, a housekeeper and now the woman he loved more than life itself, though the last had been of his own choosing. He had to protect her, but when it came down to it maybe even leaving her wouldn't accomplish that goal. How long had that man been watching him, learning his habits, his haunts, his friendships?

Long enough to go after her, despite the fact he'd tried to push her out of his life?

He raised the glass to his lips, took a deep swig and banged it back down. The whiskey burned. He hadn't drunk for two years and the stuff tasted like horse piss. The room buzzed about him and his vision did a jig, then settled back to normal.

The alcohol did nothing, however, to quell the pain in his soul, the hurt burning in his heart over leaving

Emma, or the grief over the people he had lost in the past two days. So what good was sitting here trying to drink his problems away? Wasn't he just making things easier for the man stalking him?

Christalmighty, he was feeling blamed sorry for himself, wasn't he?

He had a right to, he reckoned.

Like hell, came a dissenting voice. He deserved this. He deserved to be miserable for what he had done.

He's coming . . .

No, he's here.

For long moments he drowned in his thoughts and wallowed in the whiskey haze overtaking his mind. Images of times together with Emma flashed across his memory: walks along the river, a spring dance, her eyes glowing as she gazed at him, his own heart filled with emotions he'd never thought he would feel.

Life had been almost idyllic for a spell, but that had been only an illusion, hadn't it? One he created in his mind and one that had been taken away from

114

him just when he thought it might be real.

'You can't escape who you are, what you did,' he muttered.

'What did you say?' The 'keep was peering at him when he lifted his head and he forced his bleary eyes to clear.

'Ever lose something you cherished 'cause you didn't deserve it?' he asked the 'keep, his words slurred.

The barman shrugged. 'Lost things in my life. Everybody does. You just find other things to replace them with.'

'Some things can't be replaced.' Jim poured himself another glass, then took a gulp. 'Some things are special, once-in-a-lifetime things.'

'Then hold on to them . . . ' came a voice from behind him.

He turned to see Jakes standing there, face plastered with a grim look that was almost laughable, given Jim's current state of inebriation.

'They're already gone.'

Jakes shook his head. 'No, they ain't. Not all of them.'

'Says the man who used to steal horses.' It was cruel and taking advantage of something told in confidence but he had little control over his emotions right now.

A muscle in Jakes's face twitched but he held his composure. 'I know you don't mean that. You're on your way to drunk.'

'How the hell'd you know where I was, anyway?'

'You didn't come back tonight, so I got worried and came looking for you. Admit this was the last place I looked 'cause since I known you you ain't once come in here drinking like me and Hicks.'

'Used to spend me some time in saloons, back two years ago.'

Jakes nodded. 'I reckon you did, but that fella's dead now.'

He laughed, a booming thing that caught the 'keep's attention and raised an eyebrow.

'Nothing in my life stays dead, don't you know? 'Cept the folks I care about.'

116

Jakes reached over and capped the whiskey bottle. 'You need to stop drinkin' now and come back to the ranch. In this condition, you're a right perfect target for whoever's doing this.'

Jim shook his head. 'Oh, no, I'm not. He don't want me yet. He wants to take those around me first.'

'Then we best protect them.'

'Already have. Told Emma to stay the hell away from me.'

'You're a fool if you think that will help, boy. Whoever it is that's come a-calling, if he knows anything about you, and I'm damn sure he does, he won't leave her be just 'cause you got some fool notion to ruin whatever chance of happiness you've made for yourself.'

Anger got the better of him then, misdirected but overwhelming. It burned in his veins like bad whiskey. He grabbed Jakes by the shirt, swung him around and pressed his face close.

'What the hell you know about my life? What right you got coming in here and talking to me like I was some fool greenhorn?' Spittle gathered at the corners of his mouth and his eyes went bleary again, then focused.

The barkeep was staring, as were a number of the patrons. The laughs of the bargirls softened, their eyes going wide with surprise.

Jakes's eyes narrowed. 'I'm making allowances for what you been through, boy, but don't push your luck. I ain't about to be manhandled.' Jakes's arms knifed between Jim's, easily breaking his hold. The foreman pushed Jim back into his seat.

Jakes's gaze spiked him. 'Stop feeling so damn sorry for yourself and do something about this fellow dogging you. You took your balls in your hands two years back, do it again.'

'I didn't have nothing to lose, then, Jakes,' he muttered, emotion rising, overriding the anger. 'Now . . . now I got everything to lose and it ain't worth it.'

'Like hell, it ain't. Happiness is worth

holding on to, worth fighting for.'

'That what you're doing?'

Jakes's brow cinched. 'That's what I did. I changed my life and I got no regrets. I like the way things are now. Someday I might even meet me a woman like the one you did and it'll get better. I won't let some sonofabitch ride in here and take it from me.'

Jim leaned his elbows on the counter-top and buried his face in his hands.

His foreman was right. He couldn't let that man take anything else from him. He had to find a way to fight him, bury him permanently this time.

'Come back to the ranch, tell me what we're dealing with.' Jakes touched Jim's shoulder and Jim looked up, tears shimmering in his eyes.

'I can't lose this, Jakes. I can't. I've spent too long trying to atone for what I did.'

'Then don't lose it. Grab hold and keep holding to it.'

He peered at the whiskey bottle long and hard. It would be so easy just to finish that bottle, drown every emotion inside him.

But they would still be there when he sobered up. The man stalking him would still be there.

You cannot escape . . .

No, he couldn't. He had to face it, the way he did once before. And this time make sure it was over.

He nodded, slipped off his stool and let Jakes guide him by an elbow towards the door. He jammed his hat on to his head, walking a bit unsteady as they took the three steps to the landing, then crossed to the batwings.

The night air revived him a little. Stomach roiling, he rushed to the railing and retched. After vomiting on to the dust below, he sucked deep breaths and tried to steady himself. He was no longer used to drinking.

Jakes's hand touched his back after a few minutes and he straightened, somewhat steadier, his vision clearer.

'I'm all right,' he mumbled.

'We should go see the marshal, Jim.

Tell him what's going on. His light's still on over there.'

Jim gazed down the boardwalk and spotted buttery light coming from the marshal's office.

'No, that ain't right. Powers always hits the hay early . . . ' The words of Miss Gulliver from earlier suddenly jumped into his mind and dread rose in his being. 'Hadn't seen him all day', she had said, and that his door was locked.

'Christalmighty, no!' He started towards the office.

His boots clomped like gunshots on the boardwalk and his heart hammered, any residual drunkenness vanishing as adrenaline flooded his veins. His legs, though wobbly, steadied with each stride until he reached the office. He fell against the door, panting, afraid to force his way inside.

His hand went out, trembling and gripped the door handle; it wouldn't turn.

'Locked,' he said, as Jakes came up behind him.

'Get out of the way,' Jakes said and Jim pushed himself away from the door and to the side.

Jakes snapped out a leg and his boot heel crashed into the door. It rattled but didn't budge. He did it again, again, and at last the jamb splinted around the lock and the door flew inward.

Jakes stepped inside, pushing the door away as it rebounded, and peered about the office. Jim came in behind him, stopped, his belly dropping. He saw the marshal. At least, he saw his legs. They protruded from behind the back of the desk.

'No . . . ' he said, shaking his head. 'Please not another one.'

Jakes uttered a curse, went to the body and knelt down. His head slumped and a groan came from his lips.

The foreman came to his feet, something in his hand, keeping his back to Jim for a moment.

'He's dead . . . shot,' Jakes said.

Jim stood frozen, gripped by horror, by loss. He no longer knew how to react, how to face another death.

'There's a note,' Jakes said. 'Was lying on his chest.'

The words startled him, and he swallowed hard against the emotion balling in his throat. 'What does it say?'

Jakes turned, dropped the note on to the desk, frowned. 'One word: 'Soon'.'

He's coming . . .

★ ★ ★

The boy should have discovered the marshal's body by now, the man reckoned. He had left a light on in the lawman's office, knew Powers's habits as well as Jim Bartlett's. He had stalked the boy all day, though the boy hadn't suspected it. Watched him go into the bar for the first time since he had been observing. Things were progressing in a most satisfying manner. It wouldn't be long now before the man took his final revenge.

The man moved through the tall graze like a grayblack ghost, duster

123

rippling in the breeze. He approached from the western part of the property, drifting to a stand of cottonwoods, then peered at the darkened house. He had seen the foreman ride off in the direction of town; even if they did not find the marshal's body tonight they would eventually. A lawdog wasn't missed for long.

He moved forward, towards the bunkhouse, his hand slipping to the gun at his hip, drawing it. One man was in the building, a ranch hand called Hicks. He would be easy; he didn't know what was coming. Stupid error in judgment on the boy's part not to warn his men, but predictable. Boy thought he could best him again, handle it all by himself.

How wrong he was. Fatally wrong.

He eased up to the building, took the stairs in fractions in order not to make a sound. Peering into the window, he saw the 'hand seated at a table, flinging cards down in a game of solitaire. He uttered a small laugh, then went to the door and flung it open.

The ranch hand never had a chance. He half rose, shock sweeping across his face. An instant later the man pulled the trigger and Hicks flew backward over his chair, landing in a heap on the floor. The man smiled, holstered his weapon and backed from the building. He closed the door behind him.

It took him only a few moments to locate a tin of kerosene in a shed. He carried it to the bunkhouse then splashed the fluid across the porch and walls. Once finished, he tossed the tin to the ground, plucked a wooden match from his pocket and snapped it to flame against a tooth.

With a soft laugh, he flung the match to the soaked boards and flames *woofed* to life. Fire spread quickly, devouring the dry timber. A moment later, the entire building was ablaze.

The man watched the fire, head low, flickering shadow and orange showing glimpses of the monster he truly had become. He laughed, satisfaction filling him.

'Nobody leaves . . . ' he whispered. 'Nobody, boy. You hear me?'

He backed away, knowing they would be returning from town soon because someone would spot the flames' glow against the dark night sky.

He drifted away, towards the western end and the arroyo.

He would be back soon — very soon, indeed.

8

Jim leaned on the rail outside of the marshal's office, all effects of the whiskey having vanished the moment he'd discovered Tom Powers's body. His head was entirely too clear and a strange numbness had flooded his being.

Men milled around — the funeral man and a few cowboys who'd assisted him in carrying the marshal's body to a wagon now parked in front of the office. The body lay in the back, covered with a blanket.

Jim couldn't even glance at it. He'd seen far too much death in the short space of two days. Death that wouldn't stop until it came for him.

Soon . . .

That's what the note had said. He knew somewhere, out there, that man was watching, reveling in the pain he was causing. He was alive, impossibly, yet certainly, and Jim didn't have a clue what to do about it, how to stop the folks about him from getting hurt, unless —

'You can't run from it,' Jakes said, coming up to him, placing a hand on his shoulder. 'I know that's what you're thinking. But he found you here, and he'll find you anywhere you go. You run, you'll never be free. It has to end now.'

Jim nodded, knowing his foreman was right. 'How'd you know what I was thinking?' He didn't look at Jakes, merely stared at the street.

'Because it's what I would have been thinking in your position. Was a time I would have run from the law, from myself, but not anymore. This place — ' Jakes ducked his chin at the surroundings, 'the West is unforgiving of those who don't show it respect, those too weak to stare it down. But it's also rewarding of those who do. You want happiness, you want to atone for what

128

was, you fight for it, don't let no one take it away from you.'

'I don't know how to stop a dead man, Jakes. He's out there somewhere and I got no clue how to find him before he finds me, or kills everyone else I give a damn about.'

Jakes sighed. 'He's an outlaw.'

Jim nodded. He saw no point in hiding that fact anymore. 'The worst type.'

'I worked with enough of them back in my day. They all make mistakes, and they all get cocky. Some are smarter than others. This one, this one's obviously got some horse sense. But he's still a man driven to get even when it comes down to it and that'll be his blind spot.'

He peered at the foreman, eyes narrowing. 'That even apply to a dead man?'

Jakes hesitated. 'You ready to tell me who this fella is?'

Jim bowed his head, wanting to keep it to himself but to this point that practice hadn't done him a lick of good. Billy, the marshal, Mrs Pendergast — all were dead. And he owned part of the blame.

'He's — '

'Hey!' came a shout from one of the cowboys who had just come out of the marshal's office. The sound brought Jim and Jakes' heads around.

'What is it?' Jim asked, thinking he couldn't deal with any more trouble at the moment.

The cowboy pointed at the distance and Jim's gaze swung in that direction. He straightened, belly plunging. A mile off, an orangey glow shimmered against the dark sky.

'Christalmighy . . . ' came Jakes's voice beside him. 'Somethin's on fire at the ranch.' Worry flashed in his hard eyes.

'Hicks is out there alone . . . ' Jim muttered. Then, louder to the cowboy: 'That's the ranch.'

The cowboy nodded. 'I'll fetch a few men and we'll head out right after you.

You'll need help if something's burning.'

Jim nodded, taking a small measure of comfort in the fact he had friends here, had built a foundation. Jakes was right. He had to fight for that, but at the moment he had a more immediate concern: his ranch hand.

Jim doubled, slipped under the rail and jumped from the boardwalk to the street. Jakes followed suit.

The young rancher ran for his horse, which was still tethered outside the saloon. Behind him, the cowboy shouted for men to mount up.

He reached his horse, untethered the reins and climbed into the saddle. Jakes mounted his own bay only a beat behind.

He reined around, jammed his heels into the horse's sides and sent the beast into a gallop through the street.

His hands tightened on the reins, bleaching, and his heart banged in his throat. The thunder of his own quickened pulse throbbed in his ears and worry over his man flooded his veins.

'Not another one,' he whispered, the sound lost in the wind whipping by him.

It took only a few minutes to reach the ranch but the closer he came the more the sky turned amber with leaping flames. He noted only the bunkhouse was aflame and that brought a surge of dread to his being.

It's too late.

Jakes rode beside him, silent, his face tightened with an intense combination of anger and worry. Jim knew of no better man to have next to him in an emergency, but the strain was wearing on the foreman.

A dead man was striking all about them; the foreman knew it — and wondered how long it would be before that threat turned his way.

As they reached the ranch compound, Jim skidded his horse to a stop before the barn. He was off the mount and running for a wooden bucket inside the building in seconds, then back out to a trough recently topped off by rain.

He filled the bucket and stumbled with it to the bunkhouse. Flames raged through the structure, the place little more than kindling under the blaze. Heat blasted him as he drew close, scorched his eyebrows and reddened his skin, but he ignored it. The thought that Hicks might be trapped in the building drove him, steeled him against any pain, any sense of caution that might have made him hesitate otherwise.

He hurled the water on the flaming structure; a great sizzling sounded, accompanied by a plume of steam, but the water had little effect.

Jakes was suddenly beside him, hurling a second bucketful towards the door area. Another sizzle and part of the door was revealed.

Hoofbeats rose over the crackling voice of the fire; riders from town hurtled towards the ranch. A moment later five men reined up and dismounted. They poured into the barn, locating buckets, then formed a line from the trough to the bunkhouse, passing filled buckets from one man to the next.

Great clouds of black smoke billowed into the night and tongues of flame licked at the darkness.

'Christ, Hicks, no . . . ' Jim said under his breath, hauling yet another bucketful on to the burning structure.

Jakes threw down his own bucket, the water having cleared an open path to the door. He bounded up the stairs, keeping a forearm before his face to help guard against the intense heat. He coughed as smoke choked him but kept going, with a shoulder slamming into the door.

The door had partially burned, and caved under the impact. It crashed inward and Jakes plunged into the building.

He bounded out backwards a moment later, both hands jammed beneath Hicks's arms. He dragged the ranch hand across the collapsing porch and down the stairs.

Jim hurled his bucket to the ground and ran to them.

Jakes looked back to him, shook his head.

'He's dead, Jim,' Jakes said, straightening. 'But wasn't no fire that killed him.'

Jim peered at the bullet wound in the man's chest. 'He shot him, then set the building afire. He knew we were occupied in town. If I had stayed here . . . '

'He might have killed you too,' Jakes said. 'You can't blame yourself for this.'

'Can't I?' Jim said, voice snapping out, edged with fury. 'It's my goddamn fault this is happening!'

He whirled and went back to his bucket. He didn't dare pause any longer and think about the ranch hand lying there dead. If he did, he would come apart, and right now he needed to hold up, get the fire under control.

Men shouted and kept hauling water to the building, but by the time they got the flames out most of the structure had collapsed, leaving smoldering shards of blackened board and charcoal devils of smoke that curled up into the night, as if mocking him.

Hours passed in a blur of images and consuming guilt. After the men rode back to town, exhausted, the funeral man came with his wagon to collect Hicks's body.

When at last he stood alone in the field, Jakes having gone back to the house to clean up, Jim Bartlett fell to his knees in the grass. A great sob wracked his frame and emotion cinched his throat.

How much could a man take before falling completely apart? The thought taunted him, made him wonder if he hadn't already gone insane and if this wasn't all just some cruel joke or dark nightmare.

It was indeed a nightmare, but a real one.

The scent of singed wood and black smoke hung in the air, assailing his nostrils and his senses. He knew why the man had set the building on fire. It was a symbol, a taunt — a bunkhouse for a mining shack.

'Scanlon!' he yelled, his voice cascading through the night. 'I'll kill you, you sonofabitch! This time I'll make sure you stay dead!'

He collapsed into the grass, his face hitting the ground and tears rushing from his eyes.

Hicks had been only twenty-three years old, just starting his life. He had a gal he sometimes saw in town; she would need to be told. He would see to it the burial was paid for but it wouldn't be enough; he couldn't bring the young ranch hand back.

He'd brought this murderer to Wendell, and he would spend his life, if he lived through it, atoning for another in a long list of sins.

He pounded a fist against the ground, then reared up to his knees and let out an agonized yell.

For a dragging heartbeat, silence haunted the field.

'Come in the house, son.' A voice

came from behind him and he looked up and over his shoulder through tear-filled eyes to see Jakes standing there, staring down at him, his face a mask of sympathy.

'It's my fault, Jakes. It's my fault.'

'No it's not, boy. It's that outlaw's fault.'

'I brought him here.'

'You left him for dead, from what I make out. You can't be held responsible for some fool loco outlaw taking it upon himself to seek payback.'

'How do I tell Hicks's gal that? How do I bring back Mrs Pendergast and Billy and the marshal?'

Jakes shook his head, the burden of sadness making his face look ten years older than it had only a few days before. 'You don't bring them back. They're gone. But making yourself a target out here won't do nothing to help the situation any or atone for whatever it is you think you got to suffer for, either. It'll just give that fella what he wants.'

For the first time, Jim noticed Jakes's hand rested on the butt of the Colt at his hip. The foreman was taking no chances and had likely surveyed the grounds before coming up to him.

Jim looked forward again, out into the night. Where was he? Where was the man whom he had left for dead? How could he find him before he —

'I have to make Emma leave town,' he said, coming to his feet and turning to Jakes.

Jakes nodded. 'Not going to be easy. She loves you and a woman in love don't know no boundaries when it comes to protecting those they care about. She's stubborn as hell, too.'

'She has to leave. I told her I didn't want her around me no more but Scanlon's already seen her, I'm sure of it. He'll go after her. He's leaving her till last.'

'Meaning he'll be coming for me next . . . ' Jakes's tone carried an ominous quality.

'I got a notion he will. You're the last

one left here, 'sides me. He's got a pattern and though he's smart he's still somewhat predictable. I should have seen it before.'

Jakes nodded. 'This man — Scanlon, you called him? He wouldn't be John Scanlon from Colorado way?'

Jim nodded. 'You've heard of him?'

'Who on the owlhoot ain't? He vanished 'bout two years back, hasn't been heard from since. Reckon that's 'round the same time you showed up here.'

Jim took a deep breath, steadying his nerves. It was time he told the foreman the whole truth. The man's life was in danger and likely he was next on the list. He needed the option of riding out before that happened, then Jim would see to it Emma left, as well. If Scanlon wanted him, he was going to have to come after him alone.

'I was part of his gang, so was Billy, only my name was Frank Buckman and Billy's was Jess Henley.'

'Scanlon killed a lot of folks.'

140

'And I ignored it for a spell. I never killed no one myself, neither did Billy, but we stayed, so that was condoning it, which makes us just as guilty.'

'You were pretty young, boy. I did plenty of bad things back in my day on the owlhoot I ain't proud of. What matters is who you are now.'

'Who am I now?' he asked. 'Who would that be? A man who can't even do the job of killing right? A man who brings a killer down on the folks he cares about?'

Jakes shook his head. 'What happened?'

'I got tired of it. My conscience had been bothering me for a long spell; Billy's was bothering him too, but neither of us had the balls to say it until one day . . .

* * *

'We gotta run,' Frank Buckman said, turning to the younger man who sat at a table in the small cabin the Scanlon

141

gang used for a hideout. The cabin stood near an abandoned mine in the wilds of Colorado Territory. Both men had remained behind this day, while Scanlon rode out with two other men on a bank job in a small town about a twenty-minute ride south. Scanlon did that often, split up his men, taking who he felt was right for certain jobs.

Jess Henley set down his cards and his eyes watered as if he were holding back tears. 'Last job we were on . . . he killed that woman . . . She was with child.' A shudder wracked Jess's frame and one rattled Frank as well. 'I can't stop thinkin' 'bout it. Can't stop seein' her eyes right before she . . . '

Frank swallowed hard. That had been the last straw, the way he saw it. He had seen Scanlon kill men before, and each time it had taken a piece of his humanity and left an ever-growing hole of blackness in his soul. He reckoned if he was going to have any chance of saving what was left, at even beginning to seek forgiveness, he had to leave now.

'I can't take it no more,' he said. 'I'm leavin'.'

The younger man peered at him, almost hopeful. 'We can't leave. He'd never let us. You know that. You saw what he did to Johnson.'

Frank nodded. He had seen and that was another sight that would forever haunt his nightmares. Johnson had wanted out. Scanlon told him fine and had even given him a week's pay before sending him on his way. Except as Johnson turned to mount his horse Scanlon had shot him in the back of the head as an example to the rest that membership in the gang was permanent and nothing short of death would release them from that duty.

'We'll go somewhere,' Frank said. 'Texas, I reckon, change our names. I even got two picked out. I'll be Jim Bartlett and you'll be Billy Fredericks.'

'How we gonna do that? Our faces are on posters, an' we got no money to start over.'

'I got money.' Frank turned, looked

out a small window in the one room shack that held meager furniture — the table at which Jess was sitting, a few hardbacked chairs and five bedrolls.

'How? How you got money?' Jess asked. 'He don't pay us that much, just enough to get drunk and maybe spend time with a lady or two at saloons.'

Frank glanced back at the younger man. 'I watched him. I know where he's been hiding the money he gets from our jobs. I got some of it hid in saddle-bags in the mine. I've been taking just enough over the past few months so he wouldn't notice.'

'That's blood money, ain't it?'

He frowned. 'Yeah, I reckon it is, but I can't bring back those folks he killed. All I can do is try to help others with it, as well as ourselves, and try to atone for what we done.'

'You sure it will work? Scanlon's not stupid, way most outlaws are.'

'Doesn't matter if it works. Scanlon's been pressing us to make our first kill. You want to wait around for that to happen? Then we'll never get the blood off our hands.'

'I can't kill nobody. I can't.'

'Neither can I, but Scanlon won't see it that way. He'll put a bullet in us for disobeying.'

Jess lowered his head, stared at the cards on the table for a spell, then looked back up. 'We gonna do this we'd best do it now. Next time he's taking us and planning on forcing us into killing.'

Frank nodded. 'Get your gear together. I'll go get the money.'

Jess nodded, came from his seat. He grabbed his saddle-bags from a wall hook and a bedroll.

Frank went to the door, pulled it open, then stepped outside. He paused on the porch, his heart thudding, sweat trickling from his brow. He had his doubts about them getting away from Scanlon, knowing damn well the man would track them down, and kill them. But he saw no other choice. He would not be forced into committing cold-blooded murder. It was bad enough he had witnessed it and hadn't dared lift a hand to stop it.

That notion made his belly cinch and he went to the rail and hurled into the dirt. He wretched for long minutes, the faces of those victims as they died by Scanlon's hand haunting his mind. Judas Priest, how could he have let it come to this? How could he have made such poor decisions in his life?

But that was all coming to an end — today. Things would play out however they played out. They would spend their lives worrying that Scanlon or the law would find them but it was better than being a part of more innocent death.

He pushed himself away from the rail and staggered down the steps, his legs rubbery, nerves making him tremble.

He wasn't afraid to admit he was scared. The future on their own was an unknown, but the future with Scanlon was a given: death. Nothing but death.

He crossed scrabbly grounds, legs gaining some steadiness as he walked.

Woodland surrounded the camp on three sides, brush and trees having overgrown the abandoned site over the years. The mine shaft lay hidden behind a clump of brush.

It occurred to him he'd been damned lucky squirreling away this money. Scanlon had one weakness, though, as far as he could ascertain: when the outlaw slept he slept like the dead. He was surprised none of his men had ever put a bullet in him when he slumbered, but the outlaw probably had them all too scared he slept with one eye open. Jim had spent weeks observing the outlaw's patterns, however, looking for chinks.

He entered the shaft, the damp coolness contrasting with the day's summer heat, giving him a slight chill. But he reckoned that was more from nerves. He went deep into the mine, to a niche that held two saddle-bags he'd stuffed with cash money from their robberies.

Billy was right; it was blood money,

but Jim saw no other way. He could do little good for anyone without it and those folks it had been taken from couldn't be brought back to life. He vowed to help as many folks as he could with it and hoped that the Good Lord, if He existed, would see fit to grant him some forgiveness when the time came. Or at least forgive Jess.

He slung the bags over each shoulder and turned. He froze, his belly plunging and heart jumping into his throat. Panic, like a wave of blistering desert heat, washed over him.

'Christ . . . ' he whispered.

'Not hardly,' John Scanlon said, standing in the mine entrance, a Smith & Wesson leveled at Frank's chest. The outlaw looked like a demon sprung to life, suddenly having appeared there behind him without a sound. Scanlon was not especially old, nor especially young, his unkempt black hair falling over his forehead, but his hard dark eyes damned Frank to death.

Scanlon's gray duster swayed as he

took a step closer. The outlaw liked his kills to be close up, personal. Jim had wondered if that was another weakness, though he could not see a way to use it against the man.

'You aren't going to say anything, boy?' Scanlon said, voice low, reproachful.

'You're s'posed — '

'To be on a job,' Scanlon completed. 'I sent Jadson and Billings on ahead to handle it themselves. You didn't honestly think you were getting away with taking that money all this time, did you?'

'You were sleeping . . . ' was all Frank could mumble. Sweat trickled down his face and he reckoned he couldn't feel his legs entirely, but he knew they were shaking. He had made a huge mistake, underestimating Scanlon, and now he was going to pay for it. So would Jess.

'Sleeping?' Scanlon uttered a low laugh. 'I got no weaknesses, boy. I'm a light sleeper but I need to know the men I surround myself with can be trusted on their own. Jadson and Billings, I can trust them, at least as much as any man can trust an outlaw. I studied them, judged them a long spell before setting them out on their own. They got kills under their belt. But you and that young waste in the cabin, you're different. I could see something in you, something disgusting: righteousness, guilt, integrity. Can't have any of that. The young'un in the cabin, he's a follower. He can't think on his own but he's got that God-awful goodness in him. You . . . you can think on your own and you got a stubborn streak.'

'You just let me take this money?'

The outlaw came a step closer. 'I did. And waited. I figured I'd give you enough rope to hang yourself. You can't outsmart me, boy. You should have known better. I've been at this far too long and I'm not your regular dumbass owlhoot.'

The gun came up just a hair, then, and Frank knew he was a dead man. He had seen Scanlon kill enough times to know the man's habit right before he pulled the trigger: close, and with a slight lift.

Whatever caused Frank to react, pure animal instinct or some latent sense of courage, he did just as Scanlon fired. Hand still clutching the saddle-bags on his shoulder, he swung them. They slammed into Scanlon's gun hand, knocking it sideways.

The Smith & Wesson blasted and thunder filled the mine shaft. A deep rumble came from somewhere and a flashing thought worried him the shaft would collapse and bury them both. But maybe that would be just, because Jess would be free and Scanlon would never kill any one ever again.

The blast momentarily deafened him, likely doing the same to Scanlon. Recovering quickly from the shock, the outlaw sought to bring the gun back around.

Panic driving him, Frank swung the bags again. They crashed into the outlaw's face, and instinctively Scanlon jerked the weapon up.

Frank let go of the bags and hurled himself into the outlaw. He got a knee in the belly for his effort.

Scanlon let out a yell, which sounded muffled in Frank's deafened ears, then tried to brain him with the Smith & Wesson.

Frank ducked and the blow glanced across his right temple; darkness flashed across his mind, but only for an instant. He staggered a step, senses reeling, the outlaw's image jittering before his vision.

Scanlon's damning laugh echoed from the shaft walls like demons gibbering. Once the outlaw brought the gun back around, Frank knew that would be it. He had dropped the saddle-bags; he had no defense against the larger man.

'NO!' he yelled, off balance, but driven by desperation and the deep-seated instinct to survive and make the wrong he'd done in his past right.

He lunged just as Scanlon swung the

gun to aim, and slammed into the killer. Jamming a forearm beneath Scanlon's gun arm, he jerked upward.

He wasn't entirely certain what occurred next. A tremendous roar shattered his senses and something ripped across his cheek with the feeling of a hundred wasps stinging all at once. Liquid flowed, running down his jaw: blood.

He didn't move, frozen with the notion the bullet had gone straight through his cheek. But it hadn't. Fingers going to his face, he felt a deep furrow and the cool slickness of his own blood: a grazing shot.

Scanlon chuckled, a demonic thing.

A guttural yell of fear and shock surged from deep within his throat and he charged forward, grabbing madly at Scanlon's gun hand as the outlaw again tried to right his aim and take advantage of the younger man's hesitation. Another blast shuddered through him and he staggered back, expecting to collapse with a bullet in his face.

But that didn't happen.

Instead, Scanlon sank to his knees, losing his grip on the Smith & Wesson, which fell to the mine floor.

The outlaw, on his knees, wavered: a portion of his lower face had become a mangled mess, streaming crimson.

The outlaw groaned, fell face forward and didn't move.

Frank stared at the form, too stunned to move.

Then, breaking the spell of shock, he scrambled backwards and scooped up both saddle-bags. After kicking the outlaw's gun away, he ran for the mouth of the mine shaft.

Jess stood just outside, panic on his face, drawn by the gunfire. He started as Frank plunged through the brush covering the mine shaft, saddle-bags in hand, face spattered with blood, body trembling.

'W-what happened?' Jess stammered. 'I heard shots.'

'He's dead!' Frank managed to pant out, his heart trip-hammering so hard he thought it might burst from his chest.

'Who's dead?' Jess gripped his arm, steadying him; Frank might have collapsed otherwise.

'Scanlon! Scanlon's dead!'

'*What?*' Incredulity laced Jess's voice. 'What was he doing here? He was s'posed to be out with Jadson and Billings on that bank job.'

'He knew I was taking the money; he came back to kill us. But I killed him. It was an accident.'

The crashing notion he had just killed a man, even a bad man, made his belly twist and his soul revolt.

Jess gave him a panicked look. 'We gotta get out of here before the others come back. Don't matter you killed him. Now he can't follow us. We're free.'

★　★　★

'Least we both thought we were,' Jim said, as he came from the memory and peered at Jakes. He touched the slight scar where the bullet had creased his cheek that long ago day.

'Obviously, he lived through it, somehow. You couldn't have killed him.'

Jim uttered a small sound of disgust. 'You know, along with all my other guilt, I always carried a bit for Scanlon, for killing a man, even one like him. I reckon in some way I should be relieved I didn't, but I'm not. I wish I had killed him because living with that guilt was a hell of a lot easier than living with the blame. I brought him to this town and some good folks have paid the price.'

Jakes shook his head, shifted his feet. 'You did the best you could. You thought he was dead and you built a hell of life here, helped out a lot of folks. You got nothing to feel guilty about. We just gotta find him before he hurts anyone else.' The foreman's hand eased over the butt of his Peacemaker. 'And make sure he's truly buried this time.'

Standing now, Jim peered at the

foreman, saw the conviction steeling his face. 'You can leave, you know. This ain't your fight.'

Jakes looked at the ground, then back up to Jim. 'I got my own guilt, my own sins I need to make amends for. When I decided to ride the straight trail, I made promises to myself. One of them was never desert someone in need. That church woman long ago gave me that. I'm staying.'

Jakes stuck out his hand and Jim hesitated. How could he risk this man's life?

'I ain't giving you a choice,' Jakes said, a small smile pulling at the corners of his mouth.

Jim took the foreman's hand, shook it hard.

Jakes grinned. 'Let's give this sonofabitch what he deserves.'

★ ★ ★

John Scanlon recollected the day he'd been left for dead by that boy and anger

157

burned through his veins.

He sat on a log within one of the caves peppering the arroyo that ran along the western edge of the boy's property, property bought with his money. A small fire crackled before him, causing an eerie cavorting of shadow and flame across the cave walls. Scanlon's head was down, his hat pulled low so shadows covered his face.

He had kept that face hidden for two years, all the time searching for the boy who'd left him for dead. For all intents, he had been dead, the outlaw known as John Scanlon gone from a West that was only too happy to see his demise.

The boy hadn't left much trail to speak of, nothing substantial pointing to this section of the Texas Panhandle. That's why it had taken so long to find a lead, but that had given him time to plan, to make certain that when the day of reckoning came, it would come with a vengeance.

He'd hired a Pinkerton man to locate the man now known as Jim Bartlett, then killed the detective in lieu of payment.

A howl rose out in the night and Scanlon started.

He feared no man but the cry of prairie wolves sent fear crawling through his belly. How he despised those lowly critters.

'Damn beasts . . . ' he muttered, his mind traveling back in time.

★ ★ ★

Two years earlier. He woke in darkness, his eyes already adjusted to the dim light, and for dragging moments he could not recollect where he was.

The mine. Yes, that's where. With the boy he had intended to kill.

He lay on the mine floor, and as he gained awareness, a shattering pain throbbed in his face. The rest of his memory flooded back.

The struggle, the gun blasting. Dumb luck had saved that boy's useless life and had nearly taken Scanlon's own.

He tried to move, every muscle stiff, resistant. With movement came shards of pain, through his jaw and pounding in his skull. Darkness reeled before him and nausea flooded his belly. He lay still for a handful of heartbeats, drawing heavy breaths, letting his vision settle.

His fingers drifted to his lower face, felt the slick wetness there: his own blood.

'I'll be damned . . . ' he muttered. Somehow that boy had shot him.

How much damage had the bullet done? He was alive but already a strange heat swarmed through him. He was becoming feverish and that would mean death if he didn't find a sawbones.

He struggled to push himself up, head spinning and body aching, limbs heavy and trembling.

Shapes. Sudden darting shapes. Moving left, right, circling.

A low growl.

Oh, hell . . .

Prairie wolves. In the mine with him, likely attracted by the scent of his blood and the promise of an easy meal.

John Scanlon had never truly felt fear but he felt it now. In his weakened condition, he was easy prey for the mangy scavengers.

'Git!' he yelled, voice hoarse, but booming. The animals weren't intimidated. They had likely been circling, determining his condition for a spell before he revived and judged him little threat.

Sharp pain jabbed his leg and he cried out; one of the creatures had ventured close and sunk its fangs into his calf.

Another suddenly tugged at his sleeve, yanking his arm. He let out a grunt of pain as his arm dislocated from its socket.

He kicked at a dark shape that darted in, repelling it with a yelp, but as quickly another snapped at his side, incisors penetrating his shirt and piercing his flesh.

With a guttural sound that came from deep within his throat, he struggled to hoist himself to his hands and knees, but the animals darted in, out, nipping at his clothing, his limbs.

Where was the goddamned gun he carried? He felt around for it but a coyote bit at his probing fingers and he jerked back his arm, collapsed on to his side, then rolled on to his back.

Pain lanced his face and the scent of raw meat from a coyote's breath assailed his nostrils as the creature sank its teeth into his lower face.

An agonized scream came from his lips, and he lashed out, with one arm trying to thrust off the attack.

But there were too many, all of them emboldened by his impotent defense.

The prairie wolves converged upon him, jaws snapping, peculiar whines and growls issuing from between their bared fangs.

He experienced pain unlike any he had felt before as more fangs plunged into his face and side and legs. The boy might not have killed him directly, but the result would be the same, because these creatures were going to tear him to shreds.

A flash of light and thunder — sudden, blinding, deafening. The coyotes scrambled back. Scanlon's eyes, blurred by sweat and blood, struggled to focus but he caught only glimpses of shapes scurrying.

More thunder blasted — guns firing, he realized, flashes from their muzzles like violent ghosts that vanished as suddenly as they appeared. Coyotes yelped and scattered, some bolting through the mine shaft opening, others dying in the dirt.

Then things went black. Days flowed into nights and feverish visions of coyotes and the men he'd enjoyed killing flashed before his mind the few times he regained consciousness. Fever chilled him, shuddered through to his bones; at other times, drenched him in sweat and what surely felt like the fires of Hell. A horrid image of the boy that was half coyote, half man, razor teeth flashing, red eyes glowing, haunted him. And pain, such incredible pain, raging through his face, his body.

He had no way of judging how long he remained in this fevered state. But when at last he came from it his two men told him it had been nearly a month.

He lay next to a campfire burning outside the mine shaft, on a bed of blankets.

His men told him they had returned from the bank job to find the camp deserted and the cabin burned to the ground. Upon hearing him cry out from within the mine shaft, they'd gone to investigate. They had dragged him from the cave after dispensing with the coyotes, then located a sawbones in town. The sawbones had set his arm back in its joint and patched him up as best he could, but the chances of his pulling through had been negligible.

But pulled through he had, and when he was at last able to stand two weeks later, he had repaid his men's kindness in nursing him back to health by killing them.

He could allow no witnesses to his

living condition. The boy believed him dead and Scanlon wanted it to stay that way. It would make tracking the boy easier if he thought no one was after him.

The sight of what the bullet and those prairie wolves had done to his lower face had caused him to develop the habit of wearing a low-pulled hat near constantly. Folks would have noticed a man such as he had become, a monster now without to match the one within.

A few days after disposing of his own men, he visited the doctor and saw to it the sawbones would never tell a soul he had treated a man named John Scanlon.

* * *

Scanlon jerked from his reverie, the howl of another prairie wolf severing the cord to his past.

He stood, went to the cave mouth and surveyed the night, hoping to catch sight of the animal so he could put a bullet in its mangy hide.

He saw nothing but grassland and a dark-watered creek glazed with shards of moonlight.

With a peculiar heaviness of being left over from his remembrance, he stepped outside, peering into the distance.

No glow lit the night sky; the bunkhouse fire was out, but the damage was done. An eye for an eye. Now to wait, let it set in for a short spell, let the boy dwell on what was coming.

By this time the boy now known as Jim Bartlett surely knew he had not killed John Scanlon. By now, the boy knew he could never escape his fate.

Men never left the Scanlon gang, not unless it was in a pine box. He'd warned the boy, proved it by example.

'Soon . . . ' he whispered. 'Real soon . . . '

9

At dawn, Jim Bartlett stood on the veranda, gazing out across the blood-colored field. The sun was poised just below the horizon, painting the wispy clouds and sky with scarlet. His hand clamped about a cup of coffee, his soul trembled with the knowledge that the man he had been in his past had finally come back to confront him. He was looking into the mirror of memory and seeing a beast reflected.

A man can't run from himself, from the things prying at his conscience; he knew that now, emphatically and fatally. He could not make up for what he had done, who he had been, unless he unburdened his soul to those he held most dear.

He would do that today, tell Emma what he had been, then ask her to leave this town until he and Jakes took care of

Scanlon. He reckoned there was little chance once she knew his past that she would return to Wendell, if she did indeed heed his advice and leave. He couldn't blame her if she never wanted to see him again. But that was a chance he had to take to save her life.

His gaze shifted to the smoldering remains of the bunkhouse and he shuddered, despite the warmth riding in with the early morning. If he survived the encounter with Scanlon, he could rebuild, but he could never replace the lives lost.

A knot of emotion lodged in his throat and he forced back waves of anger, grief, helplessness. He had to focus on those still left: Jakes and Emma. His own life didn't really matter.

'She won't leave,' Jakes said, coming out of the house on to the veranda, a cup of Arbuckle's in his hand.

Jim's gaze kept steady on the burned-out bunkhouse. 'She'll have to.'

Jakes, now standing beside him,

shook his head. 'She loves you.'

'She won't after I tell her who I really am.'

Jakes let out a small laugh. 'I wouldn't be so sure. Women — they got this notion they can change menfolk for the better and you're already halfway there. She'll stay.'

He frowned and passed his cup to his foreman. 'Then I best make it convincing how much of a bastard I am.'

He stepped off the porch, went to the barn, and saddled a fast horse.

Moments later, he was galloping towards town, a strange desperation overtaking him. He realized now what was most important to him, and that was the woman he intended to save from Scanlon. He had to make his plea convincing; she had to leave. Whether she came back to him after it was over, well, as long as she was safe, that was what mattered. No regrets. Not anymore. This time he would make things right. This time there would be no guilt over killing a man. Scanlon was a thing of evil, and killing him was justice.

The sun lifted over the horizon, turning from blood to blazing gold in a sapphire sky. It warmed his body but failed to chase away the chill burrowed inside his soul.

When he reached town, he slowed the bay to a trot along the wide main street. His belly tightened as he spotted her on the boardwalk, heading for the dress shop. Even from that distance he could see the dark half-circles beneath her eyes. She hadn't slept, and that was his fault.

He reined up and hopped down from the saddle. and she looked over at him, anger flashing in her eyes.

'Why are you here?' she said, her voice hard, challenging, her stance rigid.

He couldn't blame her for being angry and hurt. She likely hated him and by the time he was done she would all the more.

'I came to ask you for a favor,' he said, his own voice hesitant. Confessing the truth to someone you loved came harder than he thought.

She laughed with a spiteful quality he'd never heard from her before — spite driven by hurt.

'You have a nerve,' she said, eyes narrowing. 'And just why would I do you any favor, Mr Bartlett? As I recollect, you didn't want anything more to do with me.'

He bowed his head, placed one foot on the steps leading up to the boardwalk. He deserved any venom she spat at him, but it still pained his innards.

'If you don't do me this favor you are going to die,' he said, head lifting, voice low and serious. 'You'll die because of who I am, what I was.'

She peered at him, taken aback by his tone, but quickly recovered her composure. 'Who are you, Jim? I've always known you were hiding something. I prayed one day you'd trust me enough to tell me, but if you want me to give you even another second of my time you best be out with it now.'

He nodded. 'My real name is Frank Buckman. I rode with the Scanlon gang.' He waited to see if the name brought any recognition from her, carried any impact. When it didn't, he told her the entire story. She listened, myriad emotions washing across her face: anger, hurt, shock, disbelief and disgust.

When he was finished, she walked to a supporting post and leaned against it, looking as if she might collapse. She was a strong woman but she hadn't expected what he'd confessed.

Hurt played in her eyes. 'All this time . . . when I thought you loved me, you were somebody else?'

He took a deep breath. 'I do love you, Emma. That's why I'm telling you this. That man, Scanlon, he's come back. He's killing everybody I care about to get even. That's why I want you to leave Wendell and not look back.'

She peered at him, lower lip trembling. 'You can't be serious, Jim or whoever you are. I have a life here. I just won't throw it away.'

'You'll throw it away if you don't leave.' He put it to her plain, hoping it would frighten her, but she wasn't one easily frightened.

'And if I do leave? What happens to you? He kills you for what you did to him? He makes you pay for your sins?'

'Maybe. Or maybe this time I truly kill him and he never bothers me again.'

She studied his face, and he could tell she didn't care for what she saw.

'You're resigned to dying.'

She was right; he was resigned to dying, as long as Scanlon never harmed anyone else again. He could deny it but she wouldn't believe him anyway.

'You have to leave, Emma. Please . . . ' The desperation he felt inside bled into his voice. 'If you ever cared about me, leave today, before he comes for you.'

She uttered a vapid laugh. 'If I ever cared about you . . . Just who was it I did care about, Jim? These past two years, has that been the real you? Or are you the man you were when you rode with this outlaw?'

'Reckon that's for you to decide. I never told you about my past because I reckoned I'd lose you, but I never lied to you about anything else.'

'And I'm just s'posed to take your word on that?' She uttered a disgusted sound. 'All this time, I wondered, why ain't he asking me to marry him? Is it me, something I said or did? Maybe I'm just not the woman he wants to spend his life with. I blamed myself. But it wasn't me, was it? It was you. All the time, it was you. Hiding the real man from me. And you were just fine letting me think I was at fault.'

'It wasn't like that. I just didn't want to lose you. I wanted to make things right for what I did.'

She pushed herself away from the rail, her carriage stiffening and her chin lifting, and wrapped her arms about herself.

'You had told me I would have understood. That's the funny thing about it, isn't it? A little trust goes a long way.'

He bowed his head, heart heavy, knowing he had made a mistake in not trusting her with his secret, adding to the list of mistakes he'd committed over the past few years. But he couldn't undo his bad judgment. There was only her future to think of.

'Then you understand why you have to leave?'

She went to the door of the dress shop, pulled a key from her pocket and inserted it into the lock. After pushing open the door, the little bell chiming within, she looked back to him. 'I understand, Jim. Truly I do. But you can just go to hell.'

She stepped into the shop and slammed the door behind her. He stood there, staring at the closed door like some kind of dumbstruck idiot.

He considered following her in but at the moment she was too hurt, too angry to listen to him any further. He hoped she would reconsider, would leave, at least for a spell. But he had grave doubts she would take his advice.

That meant, somehow, he had to find Scanlon first. Trouble was, he had no idea where to start looking.

★ ★ ★

John Scanlon stood in an alley across from the dress shop, watching the building for long moments. He had suspected that would be the boy's next play, to try to save the girl. He had planned to leave her until last, until after he took care of the foreman, but perhaps that plan needed to change now, because he had overheard the boy trying to persuade her to leave town. And that was simply unacceptable.

No, no, no.

He watched the boy ride out towards the ranch, hate brewing at the sight of him. Sometimes it was all he could do not to shoot him in the back and be done with it, the way he had other outlaws who tried to leave his gang. But that would ruin everything, wouldn't it? And this was too damned personal to throw away for the momentary satisfaction of killing him in anger.

His gaze returned to the dress shop, and his mind drifted. Pretty girl. It had been a long time since he'd had a woman — women had been the last thing on his mind the past two years. But perhaps this woman, perhaps he would take her in front of Bartlett before killing her.

Or perhaps he'd simply kill her and be done with it, then present her to Bartlett just before he ended the boy's life.

Choices. Life was filled with choices, wasn't it? He uttered a low laugh. It sure as hell was.

★　★　★

The nerve of that man! thought Emma Hanson as she stared out through the dress shop window into the darkening street. Dusk turned shadows to gray and folks shuffled off in the direction of their homes. She noticed a few cowboys

177

heading towards the saloon, eager to put on the elephant after a hard day's work on the ranch.

Today had been hell for her, trying to work though her misery. She forced back tears that came to her eyes and wrapped her arms about herself. Her heart ached and she lost count of how often throughout the day her memory had dwelled on the happy times she and Jim had experienced together.

But he had lied to her, convinced her he was someone he was not. Was he even real? Was he still an outlaw or had he really changed? He had lied, but had that simply been out of fear or was there some darker reason?

She didn't know what to believe. Her thoughts kept racing, and her heart was getting heavier with each remembrance of what they had shared. But she had been through a bad relationship before, had sworn she would never accept lies and deceit again. Was this different, though? Maybe he had wanted to start a new life and it was the only way he knew how. Was she entitled to his past? Were the lies habitual or contained to what he had been?

But he had hidden the truth from her for the entire time they had been together. That wasn't *his* past; that was *their* past.

She shook her head, confusion mixing with anger. Her lips pursed and her forehead cinched. He wanted her to just leave this town, run from everything she had built. But she could not. She had made a vow to herself, refusing to run from anything or anyone ever again; that not only meant this outlaw Jim had warned her about but her own emotions as well. She was too strong now, and she would face them, make a decision. But she would not run.

This man who was threatening Jim ... She had not heard of him but could tell from the way Jim had warned her he was something worse than a run-of-the-mill outlaw. He was something evil and if he was responsible for murdering the general store man along with Jim's housekeeper and ranch hand, then he was a monster as well.

She would be next. That's what Jim had told her. He was trying to protect her, but she had let her anger over his deception get in the way of seeing that sincerity in his eyes, hearing it in his voice.

She shuddered, his words running through her mind again. She wouldn't run, but that didn't mean she couldn't be scared. But not entirely for herself. No, she was scared for Jim and what might happen when this man Scanlon came for him. She loved him and she would not stop loving him, no matter what he had done.

Can you forgive him? she asked herself, sighing, wondering if she weren't being a fool again.

She didn't know. It would take time to sort that out, but did they even have time?

She peered along the street, gaze searching alleys and building corners where someone might be lingering, watching. She spotted nothing unusual but if this man was killing the folks Jim cared about, then he must spend time following him, observing, picking out those most important to the young rancher. Despite her anger, she knew that meant her, because he truly did love her, even if he didn't dare trust her completely.

She might have forgiven him had he come to her early on. He was wrong in thinking she would have ended their relationship. But now — after so much time — maybe he was right.

It explained everything, too. How many nights had she lain awake, wondering when he was going to ask her to be his wife? Silly little girl dreams, she reckoned, in light of things now.

You're making too much out of it, another voice inside her countered, and maybe she was. Maybe it wasn't the end of everything.

It will be if he dies.

She went to the front door as

shadows deepened in the street and folks lit hanging lanterns. An eerie sepia-blue filled the shop, making aisles of dresses appear almost alive, and she shuddered again. She locked the door, reaching a decision.

She refused to leave this town and she would not let Jim face that man, Scanlon, alone. Whatever happened between them in the end, she would do her best to protect him now. She knew how to use a rifle, so she would ride on out to the ranch and make Jim accept her help. If they were to go their separate ways it would be her choice, not one made for her by some ghost from his past. She had a Winchester in the back and she would fetch it.

She turned, stopped. Had she just heard something?

No, she was simply imagining things, had scared herself thinking about that outlaw lurking somewhere. Her gaze swept over the racks of dresses and undergarments. Nothing moved, and ghostly silence haunted the shop. The sound of her own heart's quickened beat throbbed in her ears.

'Is anyone there?' she called out, not totally able to accept it as her imagination.

Silence.

She shook her head and frowned. *You're being silly*, she assured herself.

She started along an aisle, wishing she had made the decision to go out to the ranch earlier, before the sun set, because night was coming fast and already the sepia-blue had turned to shadowy gray-black. And those lurking would find the darkness a much more suitable companion.

Another sound.

She halted, suppressing a small chirp of fear. This time she *had* heard something, like the scuffing of a boot against the wooden floorboards. This time she could not pass it off as her imagination.

'Who's there?' she blurted. 'I've got a rifle!'

A laugh answered and a wave of chills

washed through her entire frame. Someone was in the store and that someone was Death.

'You might have one, Missy . . . ' came a low voice. 'But it isn't in your hands so it won't do you a damn bit of good.'

The man stepped out from behind the door leading to the back room as if he were a ghost emerging from shadow. No, not a ghost. A demon; a demon in a gray duster and low-pulled hat. He must have come in the back way as she recollected she had not yet locked the rear door.

She wanted to faint right there, let fate take its course, but she couldn't. She was too strong for such reactions, and if she was going to die she would die fighting, trying to save the man she loved.

The figure walked towards her, his bootfalls like bottled thunder, his pace ominous as a dirge. He looked like something out of a preacher's Devil sermon.

She stood frozen, as if paralyzed by the man's dark presence, despite her resolution to fight.

'I'll scream . . . ' was all she could manage to say and she knew it was pathetic.

He uttered another low laugh. 'Scream, then, Missy. It won't do you any good.'

His head lifted and in the poor light she caught a glimpse of his lower face and the scream she had threatened cascaded up her throat but never spilled from her lips. When she opened her mouth, nothing came out.

That man's face . . .

'Handsome gent, am I not?' he said, the horrified expression shocked on to her features giving away her thoughts.

'Please . . . please, leave him be.'

'Now, isn't that just like a woman?' He stepped closer to her and grabbed her wrist. His fingers gouged into her flesh and pain radiated up her arm. 'You're a heartbeat away from death and all you can think about is saving your man.' He paused, his face coming closer to hers. 'You can't save him, Missy. He's going to pay for what he did to me.'

He jerked her towards him, then whirled and hauled her towards the back. Her spell of horror shattered and she struggled, kicked at his shin, tried to rake his already hideous face with her nails. The man backhanded her and her senses swam. Darkness clouded in from the corners of her mind. She was barely conscious of him dragging her through the back of the shop and even that ended mercifully fast.

10

The day had dragged for Jim Bartlett. After leaving Emma he spent hours searching the arroyo for any signs of where Scanlon might be hiding, but had come up empty. It was as if the man were a ghost who vanished with the daylight.

The arroyo simply held too many small caves over a large area to find a single man without some kind of solid trail to follow; Scanlon had been damn careful not to leave one.

Gigging the mount into a comfortable gait, he rode across the field towards the ranch compound, discouragement and defeat weighting his soul. He was out of options, way he saw it, and sitting around waiting for death to arrive, for Emma, Jakes or himself, was akin to torture.

Spotting Jakes coming out of the

house on to the veranda, he slowed as he approached the house.

'Anything?' the foreman asked, as Jim reined up, the soft glow from a lantern within the parlor coming through the window and highlighting the tension on foreman's face.

Jim stepped from the saddle. He tethered the horse to a post and climbed the steps to the veranda. A surge of frustration made him want to pound a fist against one of the support beams, but he merely shook his head.

'Nothing. No sign of him anywhere. But there wouldn't be. Scanlon's too smart. Always was.'

Jakes nodded. 'I searched the north area, questioned a few folks in town as to whether they'd seen any strangers about, but came up empty.' Jakes came over to him, reached into his shirt pocket and pulled free a small metallic object.

'What's that?' Jim asked.

'When I was in town, one of the councilmen approached me, said they needed a new marshal and you were their choice.' Jakes passed Jim the object.

Jim took it, turned it over in his hand. It was a small tin star. 'Reckon I don't deserve this.'

'They're of a notion you do. They want you find this killer before panic sets in.'

'You tell them I'm responsible for bringing him here?'

Jakes frowned and leaned against the rail. 'I told them who he was, and who you had been. They didn't care. Said they had faith you had changed and saw the way this was tearing you apart. They're giving you a second chance.'

Emotion balled in his throat and he looked out over the night-darkened land. The moon's stark light looked like shards of bone across the breeze-stirred grass.

Jakes laid a hand on Jim's shoulder. 'Reckon if they're willing to give you a second chance, you can give yourself one, son.'

He glanced at his foreman. 'Emma

don't feel the same way.'

The foreman's hand slid from Jim's shoulder and he straightened, looking out into the night. 'I gather she wouldn't take your advice.'

'She took it and told me what I could do with it. She ain't one to be lied to, and I damn sure did that for more than a year. I don't deserve a second chance from her.'

'Give her time, she'll come around.'

'She don't have time. Scanlon's going to go after her and there's not a damn thing I can do about it.'

'Hell there ain't! You're the marshal now, if you want the job. Nothing says you can't ride right back there and protect her. Bend the law if you have to, but don't just dig a hole and cover yourself over.'

He shook his head, though every instinct told him the foreman was right. He could even put her in a cell and guard her if he had to. 'I don't want you out here alone. Scanlon's going to come after you too.'

'Let him come.' Jakes touched the Colt at his hip. 'I'll be waiting on him.'

Jim almost grinned at the look that would be on Emma's face if he tried what Jakes suggested. 'She's stubborn as hell. She won't like it.'

Jakes let out a weary chuckle. 'You're making excuses, son. And while you stand here trying to talk yourself out of something you know you're going to end up doing anyway, Scanlon might already be getting close to her.'

His belly sank; the foreman was right. How many times during the course of his search today had he considered going back to town to try talking to her again, or at least watch over her? He'd almost turned his horse around before coming back here to the ranch tonight.

He nodded, and Jakes slapped a hand against Jim's shoulder. 'I'll keep watch. That fella comes anywhere near this place I'll put a bullet between his eyes. I still got some of that old cow thief left in me.'

Jim's features turned grim. 'Reckon

'fore this is done I'll find out if I still got some outlaw left in me.'

★ ★ ★

After watching Jim Bartlett ride off, Jakes went into the house. He couldn't deny the fear coiling like rattlers in his innards. Long removed from his days on the owlhoot, maybe he had gone a little soft in some ways, but he recollected the man called Scanlon and he reckoned that fear was well justified. He'd heard tales, and the outfit he had ridden with stayed far clear of any territory Scanlon claimed for his own.

That outlaw was hell on a horse, nearly legendary in his cruelty, his intolerance of folks who crossed him, including his own men.

The boy had picked a monster to piss off, that was for damn sure. And now that monster was somewhere close, waiting to strike, and an ever-growing dread told Jakes he was next on the list.

He was glad he'd talked the boy into

going to town to try saving his woman. He wanted the boy away from the ranch, wanted to keep him safe. For the fear in his belly, he realized, didn't just come from Scanlon's reputation, it came from making himself an open target to save the life of a friend, a boy with his whole future ahead of him.

Second chances. Like the one Jim Bartlett had given him by hiring him on to the compound. The boy deserved nothing less in return. Jim had worked hard to build a life for himself, and Jakes was damned if he'd let Scanlon take it away from him.

Jakes had lived his own life straight for the past year and a half but that didn't make up for all the cattle stealing and brand altering he had done, no matter how much he had told himself it did. But loyalty would, he reckoned, and protecting that boy was the penance he needed to prove he was no longer the outlaw he had once been.

Jakes went to the parlor window and glanced out at the yard, watching as shadows reached from cottonwoods and clawed from the corner of the house.

How close was Scanlon? Where was he hiding? Jakes swore he could feel the outlaw's evil presence, though he knew that must be simply dark anticipation, not premonition. He didn't believe in such things, though he believed in the evil of which men were capable, to be sure.

He gave a small shudder, the darkness in the room seeming to wrap itself around him and seep into his very soul.

Darkness . . . Wait. The parlor should not have been dark. He had lit a kerosene lamp earlier. And the lamp was full; it would not have gone out.

His hand fell to the Colt at his hip, rested on the handle, ready for an instant draw. He started to turn from the window, hair prickling on the back of his neck.

Something slammed into the side of his head and he staggered sideways.

'Judas Priest . . . ' he muttered.

A laugh penetrated his spinning mind. 'Planning on protecting the boy, were you, Jakes?'

Jakes fell against the arm of the sofa, his head reeling, vision blurred. Pain rang through his skull. He didn't know what he had been hit with, fist or gun butt, but it had nearly knocked him out. Only force of will kept him conscious.

'You sonofabitch . . . ' he muttered.

'You got that right,' the voice said and he saw him then, a black shape in a duster standing above him. A dark fist raised then flashed down towards his face; he couldn't get out of the way.

The fist smashed into his forehead, sending him sideways, off the sofa arm to the floor.

A boot heel crashed into his head next and blackness swirled across his mind. He was barely conscious of laughter and of the blood trickling from his mouth and nose.

The heel buried itself in his ribs. A brittle snap sounded and stabbing pain told him one had cracked. The pain, strangely enough, brought him fully conscious.

The figure knelt before him. 'I know you, Jakes. You had a rep back in the day as quite a brand artist. Pity you went straight. I never gave my men that choice. Your boss should have put a bullet in you, way I did traitors.' The man pulled Jakes's gun free of its holster, then rose to his feet, and aimed it at the foreman's torso. 'Reckon he'd thank me for doing it for him.'

Scanlon pulled the trigger. The blast shattered the silence and Jakes tried to twist away but a burning pain in his side told him the bullet had punched into him.

'Don't worry, you'll bleed out nice and slow,' the man said, tossing the gun on to the sofa. 'If the timing's right, maybe you'll even die just as the boy arrives back here. Wouldn't that be fitting?'

The man walked off, his bootfalls like a fading death rhythm. Jakes felt hot liquid flowing from the wound and knew the boy had no chance against this monster of a man from his past. He whispered a prayer, never having believed in miracles, but hoping for one just the same.

★ ★ ★

By the time Jim Bartlett reached the dress shop and dismounted a growing sensation of doom gripped him. He couldn't pinpoint why he felt that way, only that he did, as if Scanlon were somehow in his mind, darkening and manipulating his thoughts, his fears.

An eerie quiet had settled over the town, though occasionally the sound of muffled laughter drifted from the saloon. He peered up at the dress shop door, noting the place was dark.

She's not there . . .

Nascent panic clawed into his mind and he struggled to force it down. That she had left by now, meant nothing — she always closed at sundown. So why did the panic grow stronger as he climbed the steps and went to the door? He tried the handle: locked.

With held breath, he knocked, waited. No sound came from within, no footsteps, and no lantern lit.

She'd likely gone back to the boarding house where she rented a room, he told himself, wishing he could get his nerves to settle.

With a glance behind him, and a quick study of dark corners and alleyways for any sign of Scanlon, he went back to his horse. He paused. The boarding house was only a short way down the street, but his gaze went back to the shop and the sensation of doom strengthened.

He patted his horse's neck, then went around the corner into the alleyway that flanked the shop. When he reached the back, his dread increased tenfold and he froze, staring at the back door to the shop, which gaped open. Emma never would have left that door open. Something was wrong.

Nerves buzzing with worry, he forced himself to move, to go to the door.

'Emma?' he called into the shop, pausing at the opening.

No sound came from within.

'Emma?' he called again, knowing he would get no answer.

'God, no . . . ' he whispered, and stepped into the shop. The back was dark, and even after waiting a moment for his eyes to adjust he couldn't see a blamed thing. He located a lantern and brought it to light with a Lucifer he dug out of his shirt pocket.

It took only a few moments to determine the shop was empty, but that gave him surprisingly little comfort. A feeling now pervaded the shop, as if darkness itself lived there.

He's got her . . .

Dousing the lantern, a burst of panic overwhelming him, he ran out of the store and jumped on to the boardwalk. His boots clomped like gunshots as he ran for the boarding house a hundred yards down.

Emma stayed in room twelve; he was inside the house and up the stairs in heartbeats, pounding a fist against her door.

'Emma!' he yelled. 'Emma, open the door!'

'Lordy, what's all this commotion about?' came a voice from behind him and he whirled to see the old woman who ran the boarding house standing in the plain hallway near a hanging lantern on the wall covered with peeling striped wallpaper.

'It's Emma, Mrs Tuttle. I think something's happened to her.'

The old woman, who carried nearly a hundred pounds too much weight, most of it distributed across her belly and bosom, peered at him as if he had grown an extra head. He knew the boarding house matron in passing, had run into her enough times when he came here to pick up Emma for dates, but the old woman was the type constantly suspicious of menfolk who visited the women at the place.

'What the tarnation makes you think that?' she said, doubt bleeding into her voice.

His nerves already cinched tight, he took a step towards her and she recoiled. He had no time to argue with her, not when Scanlon possibly had Emma.

'Fetch me the key to her room. Now!'

The woman didn't move, her small eyes widening. 'That ain't proper to — '

'Get the keys, you stupid old cow!' he snapped, unable to stop himself.

The old woman jolted at his tone, her entire body rippling, then she gave him an indignant look but reached into her drab dress's pocket and pulled out a ring of keys. He grabbed the ring from her, locating the one with a large number twelve on its bow and plunged it into the lock. He threw the door open and peered into the darkness.

The old woman came up behind him, in her pudgy hand the hanging lantern she had pulled from the hallway wall. She shined the light into the room. His heart beat faster and the panic became full-blown.

The room was empty.

★ ★ ★

Jim spurred his bay into a gallop towards the ranch compound. Plans had changed, that much was obvious. Scanlon had stepped out of pattern, gone after Emma before Jakes; Jim was certain of it.

She might have left town, way you asked her to . . .

Everything inside him wished that were the case, but he knew Emma better than that. She was stubborn, and sometimes had more courage than prudence. No, she had stayed and Scanlon had gone after her first; the open back door told him as much. The outlaw had likely seen Jim try to persuade her to leave, and altered his plan. Scanlon had always been smart, not one to overlook any bets.

As night air whipped across his face

and snapped at his clothing, Jim's sense of urgency and dread swelled. He should have somehow forced her to leave earlier, should have never left her alone, should have protected her —

Judas Priest, that thinking was doing him no good. It wouldn't change anything. He could blame himself for a thousand things later. Right now he needed to get back to the ranch, fetch Jakes and find some way to track the outlaw before he killed Emma.

Was she dead already?

He swallowed hard against choking emotion balling in his throat. If she was, he would have discovered her body in the shop, he assured himself. Scanlon would have left it there to mock him. But that wasn't his plan, was it? Scanlon aimed to kill Emma in front of him, as a final gesture of contempt and punishment in the last minutes before Jim's own death. No one had ever defied Scanlon and gotten the upper hand the way Jim had that day at the mine. And Scanlon intended to make him pay for it in the most horrific way possible: the personal kill; the close kill. Scanlon's specialty, his preference. Only this time, it would be on a deeper level, one that meant the most to a former outlaw named Jim Bartlett.

'Dammit!' he yelled, slapping his heels into the horse's flanks, frustration building with dread. 'Go faster, damn you!'

His hands tightened on the reins, bleached white. His heart thundered and sweat beaded and dried on his forehead in a chilling wave as night air whisked across his face.

What makes you think you have a chance against him head on? he asked himself. *Last time you got lucky.*

He had no chance, most likely, but if anything happened to Emma it didn't matter. He didn't care what happened to him if he caused her death, and by bringing Scanlon down upon Wendell, he was just as responsible as the outlaw himself.

He mouthed a silent prayer, never

having been a religious man, but hoping that if there indeed was a God in Heaven that He would not punish Emma for the former Frank Buckman's sins.

In the distance, the looming black shape of the ranch house came into view. He angled left, his gaze sweeping across the grounds, the barn, the corral and the house in case Scanlon was watching. No light came from within the house and that only served to increase his anxiety.

Something felt . . . wrong.

A lamp. Jakes would have had a lamp burning. Fact, Jim remembered seeing a glow from within when he had come back to the ranch earlier, just after dark.

His heart pounded harder.

He's here . . .

Somewhere, lurking, waiting, craving retribution. And he had Emma with him. He was making it easy for Jim, taunting him. Jim would not have to track him down now: this was Scanlon's endgame.

He slowed his mount, hunching, growing more cautious. It wouldn't do to get himself shot out of the saddle before he found the outlaw. Scanlon would see him coming; there was no way around that. Things on the ranch were too open to ride in on a horse unobserved and it was too late to sneak in on foot. He cursed himself for not thinking things through better, but panic had over-ruled caution.

He drew up, hands cramped, forearms aching from clutching too tightly to the reins. He was out of the saddle before the mount came completely to a stop. He grabbed the Winchester from its saddle boot, then slapped the animal on the rump, sending it bolting in the opposite direction.

Heart thrumming in his ears like thunder, he moved forward, half-crouched, until he reached the veranda. He saw nothing move, no shadow sway beneath the stark moonlight; the place might as well have been deserted. If everything had been all clear, Jakes would have come out of the house by now, but the door leading to the ranch hung open, mocking him.

He paused, listening. No sounds, except those of night creatures and the chirping of katydids.

He went up the steps, legs filled with lead, belly cinching. A clack sounded unnaturally loud as he levered a shell into the chamber.

'Scanlon!' he yelled, stopping just short of the open door. He saw no point in playing the outlaw's game. Scanlon knew he was here. 'Where are you? Come out here and face me, you lowly sonofabitch!'

A laugh might have sounded from somewhere or it may only have been something left over from his nightmares. He swore he could no longer tell the difference.

He entered the house, eyes adjusting quickly to the darkness. An arc of moonlight sliced through the parlor windows, falling over a form lying on the floor and Jim froze. Shiny black liquid pooled about the body.

'Noo . . . ' he whispered.

Gripping his composure, he rushed forward, dropping to his knees before the body.

'Jakes, please, no . . . ' His voice sounded apart from him, as if somebody else had said the words.

'He's . . . he's here . . . ' Jakes got out, his voice gravelly.

A measure of relief came with the foreman's reply, but quickly faded. Jim set the rifle down and lifted the man's head, seeing the dark wet stain on his side.

'Dammit, no . . . ' He yanked off the bandanna at his neck and pressed it against the wound. 'I'll get you to the doc, Jakes.'

'No.' Jakes grabbed Jim's forearm, fingers gouging deep with surprising strength. 'No time. He's here, waiting for you . . . '

'He's got Emma. She wasn't in town.'

Jakes coughed, his entire body

shuddering. 'Don't let him hurt her, son. Don't let him take this away from you.'

Jim nodded, swallowing hard, forcing back the tears flooding his eyes. 'I'll kill him this time. I'll get you help.' He gently set the man's head down, removed Jake's hand from his forearm and pressed it against the bandana. 'Keep pressure on it, Jakes. Please hold on.'

Jakes nodded, coughing again. 'Hell, don't even hurt anymore . . .'

Jim rose to his feet, grabbing his rifle as he did so. He noticed Jakes's Colt on the sofa. He picked it up and jammed it in his belt.

'Where are you, Scanlon? I know you're here!' His shout reverberated through the room, ghostly somehow, trailing out into the night.

The laugh again. This time he was positive he heard it and though it did not come from his dreams it held a nightmarish quality.

'Come and get me, boy!' a shout came from beyond the door. 'Me and your gal are just about to have us a personal moment.'

'No,' he said through gritted teeth. He left the parlor and stepped out on to the veranda. From the direction of the barn, he now saw shimmering buttery light bleeding from within. One of the doors hung open; he was positive it hadn't been that way when he rode up.

He bounded off the porch, all sense of caution washed away by panic. He would end it this time or die trying. He wouldn't lose all he'd fought so hard to gain, to become.

Second chances. They both had one, himself, and the outlaw. In the outlaw's case it was a second chance at killing him, one he never should have gotten.

He strode towards the barn, stopping just shy of the open door. Easing up to the door, he peered inside. Three hanging lanterns had been lit on support beams near the entrance and at first he saw no one. Horses shuffled and snorted, telling him a stranger lurked in the barn.

'Christalmighty!' he blurted, suddenly spotting Emma in the shadows beyond the lamps. A rope around her wrists stretched her arms above her head, suspending her from a support beam. The tips of her high-laced shoes just touched the floorboards. Even in the poor light he spotted blood on her face, and her gingham dress was torn in places. Her head hung down, her chin against her chest.

'Emma!' he yelled, then, good sense deserting him, charged into the barn, straight for her.

Something slammed into his shoulder two steps into the barn. He stumbled sideways, the Winchester tumbling from his grip. The rifle landed on the floor, skidded to the left, but didn't discharge. Jim staggered and whatever had crashed into his shoulder collided with him again, this time to the side of his face.

Legs buckling, he went down, hitting the floor hard and rolling on to his side. Blood trickled down his cheek and shadow and lantern light spun before him.

For long moments, nothing happened. He struggled to focus, mind spinning. When at last his vision settled, he looked up, pain ringing through his jaw. A dark shape loomed over him, a man in a gray duster and low-pulled hat. Shadow hid the man's face but Jim knew it was Scanlon. The outlaw clutched a pitch fork in both hands; Jim knew he had hit him with its heavy handle.

Scanlon uttered a low laugh. 'I knew the minute you saw her hanging there you'd come charging in here, boy. You always were pathetically predictable. I see that hasn't changed in the past two years.'

Jim wasted no time listening to Scanlon boast. He made a grab for the Colt he'd jammed into his belt.

The outlaw flipped the fork in his grip and stabbed it down on Jim's moving arm. One of the tines punched through his left hand, pinning it to the floor.

An agonized yell came from Jim's throat.

'Not this time, boy,' Scanlon said, yanking the fork loose, then tossing it to the floor. He reached down, plucked the gun from Jim's waist and tossed it towards the barn entrance.

Jim grabbed his bloody hand, clenching his teeth against the pain. He couldn't let the wound stop him; he had to get to his feet, somehow. The outlaw would kill him just the same but he would go down fighting.

'Fact is, I'm not going to kill you just yet.' Scanlon knelt before Jim, his head still down, shadowed. 'I'm gonna let you watch me with your gal there first, then I'm going to kill her so you know before you die no one ever leaves my gang and lives to tell about it. You're going to pay for what you did to me, boy. You're going to pay for this.'

Scanlon's head lifted; the outlaw swept his hat off.

Jim recoiled at the sight of the face, an entire bottom side of which was little more than a canvas of scars. A hole went clean through the lower lip and teeth and bone showed through. Jim'd never seen anything as grotesque as that man's mangled jaw. It was truly the face of a monster.

'Take a good look, boy. Because you did this to me. Your bullet and coyotes, they ruined my face. But it ain't half as bad as what I'm going to do to you before you die. The vultures aren't going to have enough left to feed on by the time I'm through.'

The outlaw intended the sight of his face to freeze Jim, to crush his will with fear. But it didn't. It reminded him of that day at the mine, the outlaw's need for the personal kill. In a perverted way, it gave him a last burst of hope, and strength.

'Always was your weakness,' Jim said, steeling himself against the pain in his hand. His gaze narrowed, stabbing the outlaw. 'Your closeness to your victim.'

'What the hell are you talking — '

Jim moved then, as he had those two

years ago. It was indeed the outlaw's weakness, that desire for a close kill. Jim hadn't gotten lucky those two years ago; he had merely grabbed an opportunity. And he would do it again.

With his good hand, he grabbed the Smith & Wesson in the holster at the man's hip and got a grip on the handle.

Scanlon reared upward, nearly jerking Jim's arm out of its socket, but he held on to the gun. Scanlon grabbed Jim's hand, trying to wrench it free while scuttling backward and dragging the young man with him.

Jim came to his feet, his heels skidding on worn boards. He tried to gain his balance, to hurl himself and the outlaw backward. His left hand was nearly useless, bleeding, but he swung his forearm like a club and it collided with the side of the scarred man's head.

'You're a monster, Scanlon!' Jim yelled. 'You always were. Now, you're just wearing it on the outside.'

Scanlon twisted, slammed a boot heel into Jim's shin. Jim's leg nearly went out from under him. He wasn't sure how he managed to stay on his feet or keep his grip on the gun, but he did. He jerked the weapon from its holster, despite Scanlon's prying grip on his hand.

One hand already twisting at Jim's fingers, Scanlon grabbed Jim's wrist with his free hand forcing the gun downward. The Smith & Wesson blasted and the bullet plowed into the floor. The shattering sound pounded against Jim's eardrums and his grip loosened. The recoil plucked the gun out of his grip and sent it spiraling across the floor.

Scanlon released Jim's wrist, then hit him full in the face. The sound of knuckles hitting bone was nearly as loud as the gunshot.

Jim's senses reeled and he staggered sideways into a stall door.

Horses neighed in fright, shuffling about.

Jim fought to regain his senses, staggered forward by pure instinct and threw himself at the outlaw. He swung with his good hand, but Scanlon easily sidestepped. Jim stumbled past him, his swing and miss throwing him off balance.

Scanlon kicked him in the side; Jim slammed into a support beam, breath bursting out, legs threatening to buckle. He clutched the beam to keep from going down. The lantern hanging from the beam swung, and weird lights like blazing demons played within the barn.

'You can't beat me this time, boy. Last time you just got lucky.'

Scanlon stepped in as Jim turned from the beam, his fist sinking into Jim's belly, doubling him over. He then jerked up a knee that crashed into Jim's chin, straightening him up again.

An instant later, all feeling went out of Jim's legs and he crumpled to the floor, two feet from his Winchester. The two feet might as well have been two hundred because Scanlon slammed a boot heel into his face, kicking him over on to his back. Blood filled his mouth with the taste of gunmetal.

The outlaw bent over, reached for Jim, grabbed two handfuls of his shirt and hauled him close.

'No, no, no, you don't get out of it that easy, boy. I'm going to drag you over to your girl and let you watch before you — '

A shot blasted and Scanlon suddenly stiffened. A bullet had torn across the good side of his face, leaving a bloody furrow.

The wound superficial, he dropped Jim and spun towards the door. Jakes stood in the opening, hunched, the Colt he'd picked off the floor smoking in his wavering hand.

Scanlon started for him but it no longer mattered. Jakes collapsed to his knees, the gun falling from his grip. Scanlon let out a low laugh.

Jim summoned every bit of strength he had left, the thought of what the outlaw would do to Emma spurring him on. Jakes had given him an opportunity; he knew it was the last one he'd get. He dragged himself forward, grabbed the Winchester, then rolled on to his back. Agony shot through his skewered hand as he gripped the weapon, but he pulled the trigger just as Scanlon spun back to him.

'Closeness to the kill . . . ' Jim muttered an instant before the sound of the rifle shot.

The bullet punched into Scanlon's chest and for a heartbeat the outlaw stood there, a stunned demon in jittering lantern light. An orchid of blood blossomed on his shirt.

He went down without a word, pitched forward on to his face with a thunderous crash that was almost as loud as the rifle blast.

Jim shuddered; he wasn't sure whether it was from the thought of having killed a man or relief. He gasped a deep breath, then forced himself to his feet. Aiming the rifle at the dead outlaw's back, he levered a shell into the chamber and pulled the trigger.

'You aren't coming back this time,

you sonofabitch.'

He flung the rifle to the floor, looked to Jakes, who wasn't moving, then ran to Emma. With his good hand, he pried at the ropes around her wrists, getting them loose, then lowered her to the floor. She opened her eyes, the fear there suddenly vanishing as she recognized him. She clung to him, tears of relief filling her eyes. She was alive and whatever happened from this point was lost in a geyser of relief.

'We have to get Jakes to the sawbones,' he said. 'He's hurt bad. Can you stand?'

She nodded, and he helped her to her feet. Jim wrapped his hand with an old rag he found draped on a post, then guided a horse from its stall, while Emma went to the fallen foreman. Fifteen minutes later they were heading towards Wendell with Jakes in the back of a buckboard.

★ ★ ★

The next morning Jim Bartlett walked out of the doc's office and stood on the boardwalk, looking over the wide main street. The sun varnished the street with gold, gleamed diamonds from troughs and sparkled from windows.

Nothing would ever be the same. John Scanlon was dead, this time for eternity. Jim had buried him himself to make certain.

But that would not bring back Billy, Mrs Pendergast or the others who had died by the outlaw's hand. Nothing would. And nothing would stop him from suffering with the guilt of their deaths, because when it came down to it, though it was not his fault entirely, his bad choices in the past had led to the death Scanlon had brought to this corner of the plains. Jim counted himself lucky, in some ways, to have survived, and he would begin paying back the trust that town had given him.

He reached into a pocket and pulled out the star that had belonged to Marshal Powers.

'I'll try to make you proud,' he muttered. He pinned it on his breast; sunlight glinted from it.

'Is he going to be all right?' a voice came from behind him and he turned to see Emma standing on the boardwalk, the early morning sunlight shining in her hair. Her face carried the bruises of Scanlon's attack, but the physical injuries she'd suffered were superficial. The emotional scars would last a lifetime.

'Doc says looks like he's going to pull through. Jakes was lucky. The bullet didn't hit anything vital but he lost a lot of blood. He's a strong man, but he'll be weeks recovering.'

'He isn't the only one.' She came closer, put a hand on his shoulder. His own hand was bandaged, and would heal, though some of his fingers might not work fully for a spell.

'I was strong once. Now, I ain't so sure . . . '

She gave him a grim smile and shook her head. 'You were hard once, not strong. Strength is doing what's right, though you know it won't be easy.'

'That include lying to the person you care most about?'

She peered out into the street, her face tight, but understanding in her eyes. 'I understand why you did it. I'm not one to give trust freely, Jim.' She turned her face to him, eyes searching. 'But I did a lot of thinking and the man you've been since I met you has been nothing but kind and strong and honest.'

'Except for lying about who I was.'

She shrugged. 'Except for that. But life's about second chances, isn't it? Hardly anybody gets it right the first time.'

'Some never get it right.'

'Don't lie to me again, Jim.'

He gave her a reassuring smile. 'I won't. You know everything now. You can walk away.'

'I don't want to walk away, not if you don't want me to. How can I expect life to give me a second chance if I don't give you one?'

'I don't want to lose you, Emma. I

love you and I should have trusted you with my secret a long time ago. I should have asked you to marry me.'

She smiled. 'That a proposal, sir?'

'If you want it to be . . . '

She chuckled, a mischievous glint in her eyes. 'Then you best be down on one knee when you say it.'

He grinned, turned and came down to a knee. 'I'm askin' you to marry me.'

'My calendar is free at present, sir. I do believe I can accommodate you.'

'What?' he said, brow furrowing.

'Yes, silly.'

'Gonna need more help with the ranch now that I'm marshal.'

'Jakes will hire the men he needs when he's on his feet. Now up on yours 'fore I change my mind.' She chuckled and he stood, taking her in his arms.

At last he could truly lay claim to the man he had become, and bury the outlaw he had been, along with a monster named John Scanlon.